The Restless

The Restless

Gerty Dambury

Translated from the French
by Judith G. Miller

FEMINIST
PRESS
AT THE CITY UNIVERSITY
OF NEW YORK
NEW YORK CITY

Published in 2018 by the Feminist Press
at the City University of New York
The Graduate Center
365 Fifth Avenue, Suite 5406
New York, NY 10016

feministpress.org

First Feminist Press edition 2018

 This book was made possible thanks to a grant from the New York
State Council on the Arts with the support of Governor Andrew M.
Cuomo and the New York State Legislature.

 This book is supported in part by an award from the National Endowment
for the Arts.

 This work is published with support from the Centre National du Livre, France.

First printing January 2018

Cover and text design by Suki Boynton
Cover photograph by Meena Bhandari, courtesy of IPS North America.

Library of Congress Cataloging-in-Publication Data
Names: Dambury, Gerty, author. | Miller, Judith Graves, translator.
Title: The restless / Gerty Dambury ; translated by Judith G. Miller.
Other titles: Rétifs. English
Description: New York, NY : The Feminist Press at CUNY, 2018. | Originally
    published in French as Les retifs (Paris : Les Editions du ManGuier,
    2014). |
Identifiers: LCCN 2017015491 (print) | LCCN 2017025484 (ebook) | ISBN
    9781936932078 (E-book) | ISBN 9781558614468 (paperback)
Subjects: LCSH: Collective memory--Fiction. | Guadeloupe--History--20th
    century--Fiction. | Guadeloupe--History--Autonomy and independence
    movements--Fiction. | France--Colonies--Guadeloupe--Fiction. | Political
    fiction. | BISAC: FICTION / Literary. | FICTION / Political. | FICTION/
    Coming of Age. | FICTION / Historical. | GSAFD: Historical fiction.
    Classification: LCC PQ3949.2.D27 (ebook) | LCC PQ3949.2.D27 R4813 2018 (print) |
DDC 843/.92--dc23
LC record available at https://lccn.loc.gov/2017015491

To my mother

The Restless

Prologue

We are in Guadeloupe, an overseas department of France. It is 1967.

After the failure of preliminary talks between management and the construction workers' union, work stoppages begin erupting throughout Pointe-à-Pitre on May 24, 1967. Serious negotiations commence at the Chamber of Commerce. On May 26, the discussions fall apart again because of the obstinate refusal of one group of owners to raise wages even though certain managers have proclaimed their willingness to cede to the workers' demands. A crowd gathers in front of the building where the negotiations are taking place, and the situation degenerates quickly. Pierre Bolotte, the French-appointed governing prefect of Guadeloupe, orders the police to fire on the demonstrators, and around three in the afternoon, the first shots ring out on La Place de la Victoire. The barely repressed anger turns into violent confrontations at the city's center. Extra troops of "red kepis" are dispatched to Guadeloupe, and these French soldiers crisscross the city all throughout the night, shooting and arresting people without warning or warrant.

The exact number of people killed remained in question until 2016, when the documents concerning this event were finally declassified and a new report was published. The original count was five dead. Somewhat later, the unofficial statistic, the one released by the authorities, rose to eighty-seven. With the release of the documents, we now estimate that over one hundred people were seriously wounded or killed.

THE WARM-UP

1.

Émilienne is seated on her small bench, the one that actually belongs to our mother.

The small one for doing laundry in the courtyard.

The child has taken over the bench, the courtyard, even the night.

She is waiting for her father—our father.

She'll wait all night long if she has to. She won't cease her vigil until he comes home.

Not worth trying to chase her away. No way, not a chance.

That child has been worrying us for three days now: sudden tears, mood swings, a whole armory of whims.

She's put us through the wringer, and today, just as our city is descending into riots no one saw coming, her attitude is, frankly, pushing us over the edge.

This afternoon, in the streets of Pointe-à-Pitre, gunshots followed billy-club blows, bodies of the dead and wounded formed a path right up to the hospital just north of our house, and the child was right there in the middle of it.

She disappeared for the entire afternoon and didn't go to school.

What was she doing? Where on earth did she go and why? We'd certainly like to know!

She returned home unharmed, and for that, we thank God. But now, one whim has replaced another.

She's set up shop in the courtyard, refusing to leave until our father explains to her how in 1967, on May 26, a massacre was able to happen and especially . . .

Especially why her schoolteacher has disappeared.

Yes, that second explanation is the most important to her.

To think about her sitting on that small bench all night long, in the dark—and of course she won't let one of us sit next to her—well, it's not reassuring.

All those shadows and unhinged souls wandering around at night will slip into the courtyard, no question about that.

We're sure of it because the child enjoys holding strange conversations with shadows we don't see.

Up until now her whispering made the whole family smile.

To us it was merely a child's game.

But now, here she is speaking to the dead, people we recognize perfectly, as if this afternoon's butchery had awakened from the depths all those who'd been sleeping. Émilienne is speaking to our old neighbor Nono, who exited the world of the living some two years ago.

She also whispers to Uncle Justin, "Come on in, Uncle Justin."

And we tremble.

We also hear our little sister speak to *ma-commère* or "Mademoiselle Pansy," one of our neighbors, a scorned homosexual, dead as well.

You can be sure all these folks will add their two cents to the turbulent events of May 26.

After all, someone has to make sense of it.

Someone's voice ought to give clear shape to this story,

a story that should be told the way a caller calls out a Caribbean quadrille, in which each of the figures gracefully follows the preceding one:

First, *pantalon*
Second, *l'été*
Third, *la poule*
Fourth, *pastourelle*

We need a strong caller with a powerful voice, so we will be that caller—us, Émilienne's eight brothers and sisters.
We'll give the floor to the one who should speak, just as though speaking were dancing.
We alone will decide how many steps to the right or left each one can take. We'll decide when a dancer or a group of dancers need to leave the floor to make room for the next, or at what point a musical instrument will take up the story or add its sounds to another's melody in order to emphasize a phrase, mark a refrain, or signal the moment to change rhythm.
No, wait! We'll leave the signaling of the tambourine to Émilienne! Let her be the one to call out the changes, to play the *tanbou d'bas* that accompanies our square dances.
You say there's never before been a group of callers in a square dance?
Never seen until now, you say!
Then we'll innovate.
And every musician, dancer, or character—depending on whether you think we're in a novel or a dance—will become an interpreter.

We'll start with the waltz. A slow waltz, a good start, an introduction.

Let's innovate! And let's hand the waltz over to the child. Because, you see, who better than Émilienne to get all this going?

She's still surprisingly calm after everything she's been through.

And she's always had this quirkiness, an obsession with repeating the same phrase over and over again, like a special mantra: "I have no name. I have no face."

We even used to wonder if the child wasn't a little crazy. But maybe, maybe, she really does live in another world.

THE WALTZ

1.

Papa is coming.

Mama said he's on his way. That's what she always says.

(But today is different, isn't it, Mama?)

I'm seated, alone on my bench. I'm waiting for Papa.

(I have no name. I have no face.)

I'm waiting for him to ring the bell at the entrance. Today, all the doors are closed, and locked. Papa can't get in without ringing.

Papa has disappeared.

On La Place de la Victoire, I saw people running every which way. I heard people screaming.

(Mama, can I come sleep next to you?)

Oh no, I don't want to sleep next to Mama. I don't want to finish the mint drop, the one she always gives me when she's already sucked on it, when it's flattened out and fragile. The one that breaks on my tongue. I'm too big now.

I want to stay by myself in the courtyard and wait.

My bench is unsteady and hard. My bottom's sore and it's dark outside. Night has fallen.

Papa is on his way. Mama said so.

I'm waiting for Papa. I'll wait for him all night long. He'll come home and he'll ask me, "What does my little princess want to tell her Papa?"

I'm going to tell him that everything that has happened since Wednesday morning has made me sad.

I'm going to tell him that my schoolteacher, Madame Ladal, has disappeared and that no one wants to tell us where she is.

I'm going to tell him that it was a white man in a suit who scared her. I don't know why.

I'm going to tell him that I played hooky today and that I saw fighting at La Place de la Victoire.

Mama said I could have been killed, but it never felt like that.

Maybe Papa will know if I risked my life.

Maybe Papa also risked his life. Maybe he's already with my other friends—Nono; Hilaire, who some people call Pansy; and all the others.

Maybe they'll tell me if they crossed his path today.

THE FIRST FIGURE: *PANTALON*

1.

Wednesday, May 24, 1967. We arrive at our school's courtyard. Our teacher, Madame Ladal, lines us up. "We're going to our classroom a little early today. I ask you to sit down calmly."

We climb the stairs to the first floor without making any noise. We enter the classroom, we get settled, and then two people come and stand in front of the door: the principal (with her smooth wig sliding over her head) and a white man in a suit.

The white man shakes hands with Madame Ladal and says to us, "Don't mind me, children. I didn't come here for you."

The principal backs out of the door. (Did you see the little frizzy curls under her wig?)

Our teacher usually tells us when we'll have visitors: *Tomorrow someone is coming. He has things to teach us.* But she didn't say anything about this one.

He's come but he has nothing to teach us. He isn't standing next to her while we whisper. Usually that's how it goes: We whisper, we laugh, and then we calm down and listen to the adult who talks to us. We discuss everything he says, and then after, during break, we talk some more. Especially in order to make fun of him . . .

The white guy sits at the back of the class. We turn around to look at him. "Pay no attention to me. I didn't come for you. I've come for your teacher."

The other teachers walk past our shutters with their students. We can see them through the slats. They slow down and look at Madame Ladal. Madame Desravins winks at our teacher, who's trembling a little, but she smiles back.

The man grabs the notebook that belongs to Maryvonne, the queen of ink blobs. "Please, sir, not my notebook!" she says, smiling. Maryvonne always smiles.

She tries, she really does, but she can't manage to "discipline her dip pen." That's what Madame Ladal says. Maryvonne smashes her pen on the page; the nib separates and bends, catches on the paper. Maryvonne grabs the pen with her fingers; she frees it and tries to make it stand straight. She has ink everywhere, on the table, on her fingers, on her dress, on her cheeks, everywhere. We make fun of her, and she gets angry. It's always the same. Poor kid.

Maryvonne keeps on smiling, but the man shakes his head as he looks at the unlucky girl's notebook. He moves his head a little, like this: from left to right, from left to right. I see he's very, very angry, so I close my notebook. I get up, I hand it to him and say, "Sir, you're scaring Maryvonne."

"Mademoiselle Émilienne, please go back to your seat." (Why is my teacher being so formal with me?)

The lesson goes on. My teacher smiles a little. Her smile is proud and courageous, a little sad too. We answer gaily. We know all the answers. Her thirty-two students.

"Raise your hands, children." Our teacher is perfect, and we're happy.

The white man in the suit is sweating so much that he takes off his jacket. His shirt is wet under the arms. If he had asked us, we would have told him not to sit at the back of the class. It's not a good place to sit.

At our school, the wind blows in from the sea. So you should always pick the desks near the balcony, unless the teacher has made you sit somewhere else. Which is what she does. She starts by putting the best students at the desks near the balcony and she ends with the worst in the class near the window facing the street. She makes us change places from time to time. It depends on how hard we've been working, on whether we spend too much time watching what's going on in the street instead of listening. But we want the desks near the balcony, not to look at the sea but to take advantage of the wind blowing through the branches of the big mango trees in the courtyard outside. A nice little breeze, like the one at home that comes fluttering through our neighbor's palm tree.

We'd really like to tell the white man this; we try to signal to him to change places when the teacher isn't looking, but he says, "I haven't come for you."

We're not supposed to speak to him. We're not supposed to bring him our notebooks. We're not supposed to pay attention to him. So we forget him. We work the way we always work, and at the end, after math, spelling, and history, Madame Ladal has us sing: *"Manman'w voyé'w lékol, blaw-la-ka-taw, pou aprann l'ABCD."* We sing. How we sing! *"Your mother sends you to school to learn your ABCs. Tra la la la tra la."* We sing with the fear of God in us, as Mama would say!

It's a song we learned when we went to Amandiers Beach on the school bus. We had huge gourds filled with rice and covered with checkered towels and containers of lemonade and big mats so we could spread out on the beach. (Papa, you were the one who made the road that goes to the beach, right? That's what I told Madame Ladal.)

We keep on singing and the other classes leave their rooms before we do. The other teachers come to watch us sing. We can't stop ourselves. We're too happy. The teacher smiles and the man, the white guy, looks really surprised. It's true, we're usually not allowed to speak Creole at school.

The man puts his jacket back on. He's going to take our teacher somewhere. She follows him, very serious, very solemn. During recess our teacher disappears. With the white man in the suit. They divide us up to go into other classrooms.

(But what's happening?)

Madame Desravins tries to reassure us, "Your teacher is being evaluated, children. She'll be back, but right now the examiner has to talk to her."

2.

She's already refusing to do what we say!

We're talking about our neighbor Nono, who left this world two years ago, in 1965.

With her ninety-eight years of life on this earth, old Nono thinks she has priority to tell a part of this story. She wants to be the first one to speak. Otherwise, she's threatening to disappear. And what she says, she does.

She claims she's the accordion of this orchestra and that she'll play her part until the end because she knows more than anybody else here. That's why she thinks no one else has the right to speak before she does about Émilienne: "She's my child, she is."

Throughout her life she repeated that phrase, even if there's no shared blood between us.

She thinks of herself as a member of the family: "A good neighbor is often worth more than a bad relative." That's what she said when she was alive, and she still thinks it. "It's my duty to protect that little girl!"

Up till now, we thought that was our father's role, that he was the only one who could calm our little sister's nerves.

And she hasn't stopped asking when he'll come home. Next—if he really *will* come home. After that—why *wasn't* he coming home?

But he hasn't approached our shores today.

It seems his ship's still docked!

This isn't the first time Émilienne has waited for him, that we've all waited, and that he didn't come home.

But we haven't seen him since Wednesday.

And so, since he hasn't made up his mind to enlighten our little star and chase away the darkness, it seems we should give the floor to those who have been waiting in the dark.

Let's start with old Nono.

The privilege of age. Escort the Queen!

3.

As far as I'm concerned, this story about the disappeared schoolteacher is hiding another one, and we've got to go back a long way, really far back, to understand it.

I'm ready to accompany the child on this road because I know there aren't many people who can tell her anything about it. I, Nono, say you mustn't let things get lost; you mustn't sweep away the old memories, even if they're a bit dusty. From where I sit, my friends, I'm really in a prime position—on high, if you know what I mean. What disappears in the passage of time, what we usually have trouble discerning, that's what I see clearly.

I see everything: the family's intrigues, the events, the tragedies, and the shake-ups that have taken place in this country. I see it all, understand what I see, and maybe can even foresee a few things. So, yes, the child needs to hear what I have to say, and despite everything else I have to do, I'm ready to give her all the time she needs.

I get the feeling you're surprised by what I've said. But just because I'm dead doesn't mean I don't have things to do. For instance, I'm having a really hard time finding a part of my body they forgot to put in the coffin—my leg, if you want to know. This probably sounds like a crazy story, but it's true. One night I went to bed in my little house, so very tiny that you have to ask how it's even possible to lose a dead lady's leg in it . . . But let me start at the beginning or we'll all get lost.

Like every night for the more than forty years I'd been living in that house, I fell asleep on my back. I wanted to let my old bones relax a little, stretch out, because all day long I'd been bent over double just to finish the simplest task; it took me forever to walk two feet, grabbing at all the walls I could hold on to. All this to say that, in the evening, my body was tired. So, I got positioned on my back, took hold of my old Bible with the black cover—the same one since . . . Lord, I don't know since when—and kissed the Lord's words before reciting a Hail Mary and Psalm 23, "The Lord is my shepherd." When I say that one out loud, I feel like I'm being rocked, rocked gently in enormous arms. Once my psalm was over, I must have fallen asleep, because the next day they found me dead, my body already stiff and an arm folded under my head. I didn't feel a thing coming on.

With time, patience, and a little vinegar, the Tordoncan son from the funeral home finally managed to straighten out my arm. (He's a real sweetie but you have to wonder what he's doing taking care of dead bodies when he should be out finding a pretty, young, and living girl to undress!) A good thing, too, because thanks to that I've been able to keep my arm, even though it's weirdly separated from my shoulder and my body looks kind of crooked. Who knows what happened to my leg, but there wasn't anything to be done. You see, the knee was bent and hard. They couldn't get the kink out, so they had to carve up my body or else they wouldn't have been able to put the lid on the coffin.

They cut off my leg, and since then I can't find it. Imagine going through something like that! I don't know why they didn't just bury the leg with me. But other than that, they took real good care. You can't say the contrary. I can still smell the scent of basil on my body from the embalming. They plugged the holes up with wax, clove, and candle droppings. Can't complain about any of that, but my poor leg, someone forgot to slip it into the coffin. And how am I supposed to dance the quadrille with only one leg?

Dancing the quadrille is my greatest passion. You should have seen me dance with that old Gaëtan. Well, I mean, he got old, but when we were young we danced the quadrille until we were nearly dead on our feet, even if there was never, ever the slightest thing between us—other than those square-dance balls and listening to the caller cry out: "Ladies and gentlemen, time to dance the first figure, *pantalon*. Gentlemen, choose your ladies! Are you listening to me? Second figure: gentlemen, to your ladies. Time for *l'été*. Figure eights if you please . . ."

Wherever I am, between heaven and earth, I always hear the sounds of a quadrille. It's with me wherever I go. As soon as I hear the first measures, I try to gather up my skirts, straighten my back, and stop thinking about my missing leg. But what can I do? How can I stand? I don't dance anymore; I can't give myself over body and soul (what's left anyway) to the music.

What I ought to do now is devote myself to what was always forbidden to me as a woman: playing the accordion for the quadrille. I'm pretty good at it; I used to play when my buddy Étienne lent me his instrument. He'd even boast: *"Ou ka jwé byen tou bònman!"* Yes, indeed, you really can play!

But nothing would convince him to let me accompany the other musicians. I had the right to dance, but not to enter the men's world.

Oh well. I loved how that quadrille jumped! Does it still swing like it used to? It's the accordion and the triangle that made it happen. Those instruments are alert and fluid, like a long ribbon gracefully unwinding. And I loved, too, how elegantly people dressed at those balls. Back then we wore our very best clothes. You really felt like a lady, so you could hold your head high.

I hope we can dance in the Lord's paradise and that we're not just going to spend our time praying! Oh, if that music exists in paradise you can be sure I'll scrounge up some angel who'll ditch his wings in a corner to greet me like a queen—unless, of course, I run into that old Gaëtan. I so loved dancing with him!

You know, the quadrille is a perfect example of a group of people living in harmony. We would say, "One for all and all for one." You could always count on the friends you had from the quadrille society.

I really hope I can find that atmosphere in heaven. That and the rest of my body! If we must be resurrected, I hope the Lord's angels won't have to look for pieces of us in every corner of the world. I'd like to believe that, up there, He at least keeps track of all of us lost at sea, all those slaves whose numbers have never really been released—thousands or millions of them. I also pray that He knows where to find all those pieces of the dead that've been lost. If He wants to give life again to everyone who's lived on earth, He'd better put his shoulder to the grindstone in order to find them all, to put them all back together again.

It's up to Him to guarantee equal treatment at the resurrection, and to make sure that nobody will be afraid to present himself because he's missing an eye, a head, a leg, or something else!

In the meantime, since I have no idea what the Lord wants or doesn't want to busy Himself with, I've accepted the job of looking for that leg myself, and I can tell you it's not easy given all the gussying up that's happening in this city. Our narrow streets are being turned into broad avenues that'll completely destroy some of the old neighborhoods, and they're replacing our rundown cottages with tall apartment buildings. Where will we put our chickens and our pigs, our rabbits and our guinea fowl? On the balcony?

Even my little cabin is about to be razed, so I've picked up the pace of my investigation. I look under the furniture they kept from when I lived there; again and again I grope under the bed. My word! It's unbelievable how much dust accumulates under the bed of the newlyweds who moved into my place.

I'm trying not to think badly of them because both of them work, poor souls. They don't have children yet—thankfully, or else I might have to put up with their screaming offspring—but even so, they have no rest.

Their weeks are dreadful. I hear them talk, and they're saving in order to build their own little place on some land the man's father owns in Boisripeaux, in the countryside near Abymes—the next town over. They need money, and both of them go from one job to another, without even a minute to relax, except on Sundays, but then they have to go to church and visit their old father so he doesn't change his mind about the land. It's a fine little property with woods that are plunked down on hills dotting the surrounding plain. Kind of like the statue of a bride on a wedding cake. They really want that bit of land; they're dreaming of the countryside, of calm, of a big cement house, solid enough to protect them against the fierce hurricane winds. Dust bunnies under the bed are the least of their worries.

But during the day, when they're gone, I lift up the mattress and go through the closets. They wonder sometimes about the small changes I make in their house without meaning to.

I hear them argue, but I make sure not to intervene. Anyway, what could I do? Every day I swear to be more careful, but as I was never very organized while alive and on earth, I really don't think that after my death I'm going to learn to pay attention to exactly how far the bed is from the closet.

Most of the time, when they come back from work, night's already fallen. The bats have started to circle overhead, and the trees have closed up their arms and become immobile, like they're sleeping. It's so dark in the streets that even when you open your eyes wide, as if you're about to cry, you stay suspended in a kind of vast nothingness, wondering where looking stops and blindness begins.

❋

But what am I going on about? I should get back to the child and her family, a family I know very well. Let's start with the father.

He arrived in town got up like a total gentleman. A "gentleman."

That's a word I really like, even if I have trouble pronouncing it, now that I'm toothless. That's another thing they forgot to put in the coffin, my false teeth. As if somebody could use them after me. That's a habit they can't shake, burying people without their teeth. How ignorant! Don't they know that in the Lord's garden we'll finally be able to eat the hazelnuts we were denied in our lifetime? Some have teeth, but can't eat. Some have food, but don't have teeth.

Anyhow, this gentleman, Sauveur Emmanuel Absalon, looked real skinny in his suit! Yes indeed, real skinny, hardly any flesh on his bones. His clothes almost floated around him, way too big, and as they were cut from white cloth—not very expensive but white all the same (fashion was everything then)—he looked like a ghost, a real phantom.

You know there's still a photo of him in that immaculate suit, the only one that Sauveur Emmanuel wanted to keep from that period of pretty lean times when he was still proud of himself. Before he turned into a bourgeois.

He was almost skeletal, and his eyes didn't have the depth they took on later, that touch of dark sweetness in a white and pure ocean. No, in those days, he looked hungry and worried, a look he didn't want caught on any camera, so no one could see his distress. But the photographer must have insisted: he really should look at the camera, communicate something, no matter what, even distress, to those the photo was meant for. And the photographer probably assured him his family wouldn't see how thin he was as they'd be too busy being thrilled by the novelty of having their brother or their son living in the big city. Sauveur Emmanuel's father, tall and silent like a tree from the deep woods—those trees that nothing can stop from growing—would harbor a smile of surprise, while his mother would laugh and hide her mouth discreetly behind her hand. His sisters would jump for joy to see him like that, all dressed in white, serious and hatted, and they'd see in that photographic pause the sign of success.

That's the story the photographer told Emmanuel so he'd allow his anxiety to be captured on camera, while of course trying to appear in control.

From the beginning, he gave himself the airs of someone who'd had good luck, and it worked! He went very far for a boy who arrived with nothing in his hands except a needle and thread.

He's still been heard to say, "Give me a needle and thread!" when one of his children has a button loose, a hem coming apart, a torn shirt. If he'd been around at noon and seen his daughter's dress, he would've made her get up on that little bench. She would have stood there in the middle of the courtyard in the full sun while he busied himself sewing her dress back up, sometimes perched on his heels, sometimes bent over, sometimes kneeling. That's the way he is: he seems indifferent, but he's capable of great care when he feels like it, or when he wants to show off in front of the mother.

She'd been his apprentice, and at first he didn't even notice her. And if he did, he didn't mention it. He wanted to marry the daughter of a lawyer. It was his friend Bèze who convinced him that was a bad idea. "When you don't have any customers for a month or two and when times are hard, those kinds of people will never forgive you, and they won't help you out either. Be a little more modest in your thinking!"

That's what Bèze said and that's when Emmanuel started paying attention to Emma, the child's mother. Before that she'd just been "the girl" who'd basted the suits he'd cut, ironed the seams, and made the deliveries.

Now that Emmanuel has sold his tailor's shop and launched into construction, his wife says she hates sewing. But I know that's not true. I think she has a dressmaker come over just because it exasperates her husband: "Who is this woman who won't even sew a little dress for her children?"

See, he doesn't know she's the one making all the clothes. She waits for him to leave before the fittings; she walks around her children—taking in a seam here, measuring there—perched on the same little bench in the courtyard. "Raise your arms, don't move, you'll make Mama stick you with her mouth full of pins." "It needs a pocket. I'm going to add a pocket." She wraps the measuring tape around her neck. "I wanted to make it sleeveless, but I didn't cut enough cloth out of the bodice." She puts the scissors in the pocket of her apron.

She waits for her husband to leave, and then she looks for labels to sew into her designs to make it seem as if she'd bought them. She uses labels from other clothes because it drives him crazy: "Who is this woman who won't even sew a little dress for her children?"

"So you want me to make dresses out of dish towels?"

They argue all the time about tailoring.

All this to say that the wife is a former employee still rebelling against her boss. You should know that, in those days, even the least important black boss had an attitude.

One day I heard her call him a slave driver.

I thought she'd overdone it with that word—slave driver. It's true he acted like a big man in his little suburban workshop, and that kind of arrogance is still part of who he is. Always will be. He called his workers idiots, deadbeats, niggers—and they hated him. But calling him a slave driver is really overdoing it. Don't people know what words mean?

4.

When our teacher comes back, our joy has disappeared. It's just like Marlyse, who's a Jehovah's
Witness, says: "Joy has withered away, away from the
sons of men."

The first thing to know, Papa, is that Madame Ladal
arrives late that afternoon. That's really strange. You
should know she's never late.

We ask her, "Why are you out of breath?"

She doesn't answer.

She calls us by our last names like when she takes
roll: from Absalon to Zakarius. But normally, in class,
she always uses our first names. She makes us come
to her desk, one by one, and she hands out our report
cards.

"But madame, you always give us our report cards
the last Wednesday of the month. Today's only the
twenty-fourth."

"Get them signed tomorrow, Thursday, and bring
them back on Friday." Normally on the Saturday after
report cards, we come to school to clean our desks. We
scrape off the ink stains, we wash the inkwells, and then
we have finally earned our prizes.

"Why are you handing out the report cards early?"

This May has been really strange. Our teacher has been nervous all month long, and I even failed composition. I'm ranked thirty-one out of thirty-two students.

I don't want to tell anyone at home because Émile will make fun of me: "We're going to laugh real hard when our father's little princess has to repeat a grade."

All because I failed the dictation! I tried to erase my mistakes and rubbed my paper with the hard side of the eraser, but it left blue marks. So I rubbed even harder and made a hole in the paper. I tried to recopy it but wasn't able to finish, and I didn't get to answer any of the questions.

Émile is going to make fun of me: "Her first zero in spelling—Papa's little girl."

And I'm afraid of disappointing my mother. She gives us practice dictation every Thursday and Saturday morning when we've finished cleaning our assigned part of the house. I'm in charge of the blue bathroom.

I know I don't deserve a prize. Books, dolls, those plastic tumblers that collapse and can be stored in a little round box—they're not for me.

I really wanted one of those tumblers, but not a doll. I hate them and they scare me. Annie will end up with the tumbler that everybody wants because she's first. (Normally, "Émilienne is first, Annie second.") I'll just get the red blotting paper to remind me of my composition's "awful ink spots."

*

After she hands out the report cards, our teacher opens a cupboard she calls "our own library," where all the books she's brought from home are kept.

Normally, she only opens the cupboard on Saturdays. Every Saturday, we turn in the books we've borrowed and read the first few pages of other novels and stories.

We're supposed to make our choices in silence, but we whisper all the same, "Which one did you like?"

It's forbidden to argue. Everyone is supposed to get a chance to look at each book (but I've already chosen mine).

Our teacher doesn't want to see us forming any groups by neighborhood, courtyard, or skin color. Every time we invent little excuses ("Pauline is too poor"), she dismisses them calmly, without punishment.

*

Wednesday, after her evaluation, after the report cards, she leads us to the cupboard, takes out all the books, and puts them on a table. As she does this, we all stare openmouthed.

She stacks the books into little piles, thirty-two little piles, gathered with no rhyme or reason, two books or three books to a pile. She puts a blue ribbon around each, thirty-two blue bows. She lines them up on another table and asks us to come up, in alphabetical order.

First name, first pile, second name, second pile, until nothing's left on the table.

Nobody asks the right question: "Why are you doing this, teacher?"

Only: "What did you get?" or "Can we trade?"

※

For once, there isn't a first or last place. I'm not going to say anything. I won't say anything. I'm not thirty-first of thirty-two students.

I can show my books, my prize, first. And afterwards, but only afterwards, I'll admit the truth about the report card—*n'avoue jamais, jamais, jamais, jamais*—and about my ranking and having failed dictation. I tell myself somebody's going to have to sign the report card, even if it means I'll get yelled at.

5.

You're thinking that old Nono talks too much, aren't you?

But if I were to tell you the story of my life, my modest life amounting to not much at all, it would be obvious that every life, as mediocre as it may seem, can teach us something about history, about difference, about exclusion and illusion. I could tell you a whole lot of truths, and you'd see that the story of the disappeared schoolteacher is only a fine mist, a *fifine*, compared to what rained down on our heads when I was young. And cross my heart, if I'm lying, I'll die a second time.

You have to realize that, to know what happened before, you have to look behind.

1967. They're in 1967 and they don't have a clue about what happened in the past! They don't see how the suffering and the tribulations they're experiencing now are connected to what happened before.

Because her teacher, her pretty little mulatto teacher . . . How do I know she's mulatto? From the child herself, when she was speaking to her sister Emmy: "We like to touch her hair . . . !" I've never seen that child come touch the old white hair under my head wrap. Too hard, maybe, too wired, as they say. In this world, you only touch "good" hair!

Anyhow, that teacher is lucky to have only disappeared. Maybe they sent her to another school or to another country. Who knows? Maybe she's already crossed the ocean or is about to.

But before that, I mean way before, what do you think they would've done with her?

Yeah, nobody asks that question! I could tell you things, but I'd be accused of always bringing up the past. "*É wè finn épi sa!*" That's what they say, "Oh yes, my dear, you have to stop that!"

Standing here on just one leg, I don't feel like shutting up, because when I was a child, not only was I tossed into the hands of an old established family but they tried to marry me off! They wanted to pick the man I would wed.

I worked at their house all day long and all night too. You should've heard them talk about how I was part of the family, and what would they do without me, all that usual crap. While they were still in bed, I was already up, and when I went to sleep, they'd already been in bed a long time. In any event, school was never an option for me.

Just let me continue: one fine day my employers decide to marry me off—as if nothing had changed at all! Because that had already happened to my mother and to my mother's mother before her.

I was twenty-five years old, and they'd started to worry I was getting too old to get married. Old—that sure makes me laugh when you know I didn't die till I was ninety-eight! They had no idea I'd last for almost one hundred years. Hah!

Well, they brought this guy around, a much older man, at least forty. I can't tell you his exact age, but let's just say he was no spring chicken! They invited the two of us to eat with them.

Even I couldn't believe it; they gave me the day off! I hadn't cooked, I hadn't done the housework, not a thing. They hired somebody else's services. I wonder if it wasn't even my cousin who came in to substitute.

They told me to put my white dress on. A white dress that had belonged to God knows who and that they'd given me to wear until it fell apart.

That man and I were fed like royalty, and after lunch they allowed us to stroll alone on the plantation. Cacao beans. A beautiful cacao plantation that the 1929 hurricane razed to the ground—just like what happens to the hair on a boiled pig!

A stroll through the plantation, like a real lady with that man at my side . . . But we had nothing to say to each other. I'd never seen him before, and he'd never seen me. Not too ugly, that fellow, not ugly, but hungry, ready to take advantage of any situation. He was looking at the plantation like it'd belong to him one day. He stared at the mango trees. That year there'd been so many mangoes we didn't know what to do with them all. So many that, even before the trees had finished bearing all their fruit, new little white flowers were already sprouting from the ends of the branches. And he, that fiancé they'd found for me, wanted to gather mangos. I said no. I thought we were already too much in their debt. We had to have some dignity.

And then, at some point, that so-called fiancé moved

a little way off from me. I was tired of the whole thing: the white dress, the shoes, my stomach full to bursting, the stroll in the sun. I'd stopped and sat down, but he'd kept on going. Not too far, but I couldn't see him anymore. And all of a sudden, I wondered where he'd gone! I couldn't tell how long he'd been missing; I'd even forgotten what he looked like. I got up to look for him and found him crouching behind a tree eating an apricot. A big fat apricot with a double pit. You know how big our apricots can be, but still stay sweet and juicy.

That guy had just eaten lunch: a starter, a fish course with green peas, a meat course, rice and pasta, dessert—sorbet and all the rest—but he was still afraid of not having enough. Always afraid of not having enough! So when he saw the apricot on the tree, really fat and ripe, he didn't think. He just hid, so he could eat it.

At the time, I thought it was just about that, about not having enough. But since then I've dwelled on it, and I've come to the conclusion that those white folks set us up to have only one idea in our heads: the idea of having more than our brothers and sisters, of being above them, ready to sell them yet again for a fat apricot with a double pit. I couldn't see myself with someone like that for a whole lifetime. He would've eaten the stars out of my eyes! So I said no—no wedding, and enough of working for them! Enough of being a maid for those folks! I left for La Pointe; I left Basse-Terre. Yeah, I'd been living with that family in Basse-Terre.

That was what it was like in those days, and sometimes even worse. I was lucky. They were good but too good, a kind of goodness that weighs on you. You have to understand what it was. A kind of fake goodness, nicey-nice, where you always end up feeling guilty. You can't live your own life with people like that. You're always running, chasing after a sense of equality.

6.

We're happy with our books, but it's still a really strange day. Our teacher leaves the room; she abandons us after handing out our prizes. "Read silently; don't make any noise. I'll be back."

We behave ourselves. Nobody pinches anyone; nobody tries to grab someone else's book. *Absolute calm*, as she likes to say. We even smile, to reassure her.

"Of course, teacher, you can count on us."

"Have we ever not done what you told us?"

"We'll be good."

"I'll make sure things stay quiet in this classroom!"

But all this is making us sick to our stomachs. Nothing's what it's supposed to be on Wednesday, May 24.

❋

The truth is, when she leaves, we all start to whisper:

"A week ahead of time."

"What are these prizes all about?"

"Maybe she's sick?"

"Maybe she's going to die."

"Stop saying stupid things."

"Doesn't she seem a little uptight today?"

"No hugs."

"And she got really upset."

"Like at the beginning of the month."

Tanya, yes, it's Tanya who murmurs something: "I'm afraid."

Elizabeth yells, "It's your fault, Moësa and Lycaon."

"What did we do?"

"You had a fight in the courtyard."

"That's history!"

Papa, we call each other by our last names because we're mad. Everybody's mad. But why?

Moësa and Lycaon protest, "It's always our fault."

I don't want us to quarrel. "Say you're sorry, Elizabeth. You hurt their feelings."

"I'm sorry."

"Now let's just shut up and wait."

⁂

When our teacher returns, she has a tray in her hands and a basket full of bottles and aluminum tumblers in every color you can think of hanging from one arm.

"Our concierge, Madame Parize, made a cake for us. For a little celebration, our last celebration together."

"Teacher, teacher, what are you saying?"

"Stay calm, children. Calm down. I have to tell you something. The man who came this morning—"

"That white guy!"

"That's not polite, Émilienne, don't say 'that white guy.' It's not because he's white. He thinks that—"

Elizabeth repeats, "That white guy."

Madame Ladal sighs and then says, "Children, I must leave you. I'm not sure when. But by the end of this month, for certain, I won't be here with you any longer. That's why I gave you your report cards and your books. They belong to you now, but I hope you'll continue exchanging them among yourselves. Don't ever lose your love for books."

7.

Since I've been dead, I've noticed that on the way home from school little girls linger all by themselves on La Place de la Victoire, and nobody pays any attention to it. I notice, too, that their sadness, the tears running down their cheeks, doesn't bother anyone, not even their mothers, who, after the first incident, tell themselves it's just because fathers spoil their daughters.

These days, the trees on La Place—the ones used to watching children play after they leave school, the ones who know their secrets—those very same trees, the sandbox trees on La Place de la Victoire whose carpels sound like the beautiful crowing of a rooster, lean towards one another and intertwine their leaves. Cock-a-doodle-do! I can feel that those trees—having borne the weight of hanged bodies for days on end—are anxious. They're whispering that there's a lot more than childish fancy to this story of the vanished schoolteacher; somebody should help investigate, help the little girl sitting alone in the dark who's waiting for answers to all her questions.

And I, too, ask if it's possible in such a small country for someone to disappear just like that—not even one of those people that everybody hates (and by God who cares if they leave in chunks, devoured by dogs or carried off by the sea and reduced to a kind of sticky green algae that fish like to eat).

No, we're talking about a person some thirty-two children love. How is it possible not to care about that?

Things really have changed these last two years, because in the old days, at the least sign—a door that's still closed in the morning, an outside light that stayed on all night over an open door, the sound of coughing coming from a rear courtyard—we'd all run over to ask, "Hey, neighbor, what's going on?" or "It looks like you've kept watch all night," or "Marguerite, are you sleeping or what? Why haven't you opened your door this morning?"

Together we have to find out the reason behind the teacher's disappearance!

That child, poor little devil, thinks her father can explain the whys and wherefores of the matter. She's planning to talk to a man who might not even give her the time of day, a show-off whose story she doesn't even know, the story of a voyage that made him what he is today: somebody thirsty for social recognition, or rather, somebody who submits to the desires of the powerful. A man who always dreamed of being treated like a prince, and besides, wasn't that exactly how it was with all his sisters scurrying around?

A prince! Princes don't really bother with lowly subordinates. Does the child understand that? A prince come to town to lose himself there after having left the bush behind, who sees himself as a maharaja emerging from the forest on an elephant's back. That's at least how his daughter imagines it! That child reads too many books. Elephants, princes and princesses, servants and slaves, everything gets all mixed up—books and reality.

We need to get back to common sense: the child's father may have used his own two feet to get to town, even if such a journey seems impossible, forty or sixty kilometers, maybe even more. But whatever the distance, it's a lot to cover on foot if, in addition, you're bringing with you a bunch of things that've been poorly wrapped—just newspaper and string. And nostalgia weighs a lot as well, and only gets heavier the closer you get to town, as home gets farther away, as the noonday sun makes even the trees and the shadows of their branches disappear. Sure, you did right by leaving at the crack of dawn, but the sun always catches up with you on the way. It's honestly pretty cruel.

I can't remember anymore how Émilienne's father, Sauveur Emmanuel Absalon, managed to get far enough away to land where we were. I have to work at remembering. Maybe he took the dinghy that used to ferry people between Bouillante and La Pointe. Maybe we should imagine some old white guy giving him a ride because his mother was in service to him, or maybe it was his auntie who was the servant, or a neighbor who dared ask the guy for a favor, just a *tanprisouplé*, whispering a little prayer to secure the car. "For Pointe-à-Pitre, sir. He's a very good boy, very serious."

Yes, I think that's it. The father came to town in a car, seated to the right of an old man with his mustache and ivory-colored hat, in an old black jalopy that couldn't go more than thirty kilometers an hour and that, chugging along, took its time on the road, apparently admiring the placid mountains right after Capesterre. Yes, I see him there, seated in a motorcar that spluttered its way to Goyave, barely pulled itself together in Petit-Bourg, and slowly picked up speed before chewing up the last flat kilometers from Baie-Mahault onwards.

⁂

That's how we saw him come to town.

A prince come up to the capital . . . He already had the look.

One day we saw him arrive in the commune of Les Abymes, the outer ring, our outskirts, a cesspit unashamed of its canal—that dirty stream between the grass and the sidewalk, covered by a succession of blackened planks thrown here and there to form a bridge over the brackish, stinking water.

I was sixty-eight years old at the time; he was maybe twenty-four. I could've been his grandmother, because in those days we already had children when we were fourteen or sixteen. Even if I'd had a child at eighteen and my child had followed suit, I would've still been a grandmother.

Yeah, I could've been his grandma, and I was one of the first to greet him when he showed up from nowhere. Really from nowhere, because back then Bouillante was a backwater, with only woods and thickets. And why am I saying "back then"! Even today, in the year of our Lord 1967, Bouillante is still the place where dogs bark out their asses.

Even worse, Emmanuel came out of the Bouillantine woods—the forest of the forest, you might say. No running water and no electricity, just a river below the house and oil lamps—but we don't need to go over all that. It's old news. He showed up from nowhere with the clear intention of becoming the greatest fashion designer in Guadeloupe, a kind of Jean Patou, the man who created Joy, "the most expensive perfume in the world."

That's what the advertisements claimed, and everybody was speaking about Patou, the fashion designer who'd become a perfume maker. The child's father imagined himself climbing the ranks, from suburban tailor to fashion designer, finally with his place in the sun. He saw himself in his workshop helping great ladies choose what they wanted from his collection, all of it archived in a huge catalog.

And though he changed professions, he was never able to completely rid himself of the vestiges of his dream of becoming a great fashion designer. You know, under the staircase, only a few feet from where the little girl is waiting on that bench, lie hundreds of notebooks, samples of cloth the father still prides himself on. The mother yells at him almost every day about the mess under there.

The mother: "It's attracting mice. The little nasties are having a wild party in your samples."

The father: "Which just goes to show you, it's only mice who understand me."

It can go on like that for hours. Then the mother tries to throw all his sample books (which, it's true, stink of mold) into a big box, and her husband lunges at her, violently pushing her away in order to protect the precious cloth he stacks by category and in alphabetical order: alpaca, Bedford cord, cashmere, chenille, cotton . . .

The mother clutches a pail of cold water, adding in several capfuls of bleach. Donegal tweed, drill, felt . . . He's sitting on the ground, his samples between his legs. He holds the cloth between two fingers, weighing it, considering its quality, caressing it.

Flannel, gabardine, Harris Tweed, linen (sheer), madras . . . She takes a step forward, empties the pail on the ground, and manages to soak his behind. He doesn't move.

Mattress ticking, military cloth, moleskin, nylon, percale, pinstripe, poplin . . . She seizes a broom and energetically sweeps the floor, hitting him every time the broom gets too close. She sweats; her upper arms flap a little (she's already forty-five years old).

Tailor's cloth, tweed, velvet, quilted velvet, Vichy fabric, wool . . . He lines up his sample books against the wall, packs them together so they won't tumble down, turns around, and viciously pushes his wife away before hiking up the pants that have fallen to his hips. Then he leaves.

His wife mutters complaints; the children laugh.

This scene plays out pretty often, but he does lose from time to time because, knowing almost everything about him and his ambition, his wife is skilled at hurling the most personal of insults.

He can't stand it when she calls him "a fake Patou, a loser."

※

When Émilienne's father arrived in La Pointe in 1936, Jean Patou had just died of apoplexy. It's strange, isn't it? One moment a person is talking to you, and a second later, everything stops in his head and he dies, or everything slows down: thought processes, gestures, speech.

Anyway, Patou was the father's inspiration, a kind of distant relation—at least that's what he claimed.

The truth is, Patou had served with the Zouaves during World War I, while Emmanuel's uncle, Lord knows why, was stationed in the Dardanelles with the Allied Army of the Orient. The two men ran into each other there, and Patou, a captain, couldn't stop talking about what he wanted to do once the war was over: he would dive into fashion, women's clothing, haute couture. "You mustn't be afraid to act." When you've come so close to death, you can't waste time by hesitating.

In short, the uncle was captivated. So the day when the first creations of the man who was to become Emmanuel's "mentor" began to appear in magazines like *Madame*, the uncle—what was his name?—was proud to tell his nephew (the only boy in that whole pack of kids, and his boy too because he had no children) that Jean Patou was ALSO HIS UNCLE. He never stopped saying it: "When you have such a celebrated relative, you can't waste away in the forests of La Côte-Sous-le-Vent. By God, I tell you, dear nephew, Pointe-à-Pitre is yours for the taking!"

In 1936 the nephew decides to relocate to the big city. He's learned to sew from a modest tailor in the village of Bouillante. He has talent, a lot of talent, and that same year, Jean Patou suffocates and dies.

The uncle and the nephew interpret "Uncle" Jean Patou's death as a sign for his disciple from afar to rise up and take his place. So there Emmanuel is, arriving in La Pointe dressed just like Patou: suit, hat—and if he'd dared, a cane, too, and even three-pieces. But you have to admit that, in Bouillante, it's a little too hot for a jacket *and* a vest.

8.

The cake isn't cooked enough. The middle is soggy, too heavy.

Sylvine murmurs, "It's a *doucoune*. We can't eat it." Everybody giggles.

It's not the right moment for a soggy cake. We can't appreciate it at all; we're too miserable. You can eat almost anything with a little joy in your heart. *Just sprinkle a little joy on anything that's bitter or tasteless.* (That's what you always say, Papa, especially when Mama gives us magnesium salts to clean us out.) But there's nothing to be done for that disgusting cake. It's too late to sprinkle anything on it.

We nibble on the edges of our pieces of cake and then throw what's left back on the tray. And we wait for the bell. Nobody speaks. We keep our arms crossed on our desks, like when we're being punished. Our book bags are on the floor; the prizes are on our desks, next to white inkwells stained with violet ink spots.

"Are you sulking?" She dares ask us that, Papa! Are we sulking? Of course we are. It's her fault. She's betrayed us!

We watch her walk back and forth between the cupboard and her desk. She empties the cupboard calmly and puts all the work we've done from October to May on top of her desk. Our herb collection, all those colored rocks and birds' feathers from our lessons about nature, and the yellowed breadfruit leaves we designed, even the makeshift paper cubes we made and got graded on. (Do you remember how much time I spent in our courtyard, Papa, bent over the blue table tearing up paper because I couldn't figure out how to make that cube?) And odds and ends of embroidery she made us glue onto white paper: the chain stitch, the chevron stitch, the feather stitch, the herring stitch, the overcast stitch, and—the hardest of them all—the ladder hem.

Even Mama said to me, "Soon you'll be able to embroider *my* sheets."

Our teacher spreads out our whole year on her desk: rolls of tracing paper, sheets of bright Canson drawing paper—all the colors you can think of—stickers that have escaped from their package and created a little trail of colored spots between the cupboard and the desk. We watch them fall without moving a muscle; no one picks up the stickers. We've decided to let her handle this sudden departure all on her own.

"Oh yes, there's this too," she says.

And she hands us back our plastic corks, the ones we'd recycled from the Coeur Volant wine bottles. We were supposed to cut the corks in two and keep the fat part to cover it with wool for the table runners we were making.

"Sunday is Mother's Day. You should try to finish your runners. I'll give these to you. You should use your free time on Thursday to finish the project."

We don't say anything.

The bell rings.

"Make sure you pull the yarn tight, and don't leave any space. You shouldn't be able to see the plastic. And make sure you get your report cards signed. See you on Friday, children."

And we say nothing at all.

꙰

It seems everybody already knows she's leaving. The concierge with her cake; Madame Desravins, who tried to make us feel better; Madame Gaspésie, the principal. Everybody.

But nobody is telling us why she has to leave. How can we find out why she's leaving and where she's going? Maybe she'll tell us on Friday.

When we go past the concierge's loggia, Madame Parize shouts out, "How are you children doing?"

Somebody insults her. *"Ou two makrèl, Parize!"*

And then we escape, crossing rue Duplessis as fast as we can, right in the middle of traffic. We run until we get to La Place de la Victoire.

We've changed; we know we're not the same little girls. We would never have done this before: insult the concierge, tell her to mind her own business, and run wild. Like cattle set loose on the savanna. That's what Madame Ladal always warned us about: "Don't start running in the street, like cattle set loose on the savanna."

May 24, 1967. Remember that date, Papa, because that was when Madame Ladal's good students, the best second-grade class in the Dubouchage Elementary School, ran across La Place de la Victoire like a bunch of crazed animals while Madame Parize went in search of the principal, yelling the whole time, "Who said that? Who said that? I'm telling the principal."

Rushing into the streets, we don't wait for our teacher; we don't carry her bag right up to her pretty wooden house on La Place, a house with gingerbread cutouts all around the roof.

Normally, we walk a little ahead of her. We hurry ahead and then wait for her in front of her door. This time, since we didn't wait, we don't stop. And she isn't following us like she normally does, a few feet behind with the other teachers who talk nonstop, while she listens in silence, smiling.

She's not with the other teachers.

Maybe she's no longer part of the teaching corps at Dubouchage Elementary. Maybe she's already moved elsewhere in her head, already turned her back on us.

Maybe she isn't worried about us at all.

So we run across La Place like mad cows, and she doesn't even give a darn. (See, Papa, I said *darn* like you told me to, not *damn*!) Maybe she doesn't give a darn so much that she doesn't even see all the men who're at La Place, many more than are normally gathered at "the senate," as Émile calls it. That term makes Mama laugh, but you get all riled up, Papa. You think it's stupid to call their gathering the senate. You say, "The senate is serious business."

But a senate on La Place de la Victoire, where men discuss problems or talk about sports, really does exist. And when we leave school on Wednesday, there are lots of people there. Old men and young ones too.

Every afternoon, as a rule, young men flirt with all the girls. "*Psittent*, what a beauty!" And they wink at us. But today at the senate everybody is really serious. No winks, no "*psitt*," no "*Ay!? Mi bel ti moun!*"

Everything is upside down.

Marlyse, the Jehovah's Witness, says, "Joy has withered away, away from the sons of men."

And just like every time she says that, we burst into laughter.

9.

Let me tell you how the first suit the child's father ever made got him involved with the communists, even if he didn't plan it that way. And why he stayed, even if you'd never think he would, and even if he never attended the big meetings at the Mutualité or participated in a cell. He just couldn't get away from them. What happened is, his first customer was too poor to buy himself a suit, so he decided to pay Emmanuel in speeches and propaganda sheets until he had enough to give him real bills. Try to feed your family with that! But Emmanuel read what he gave him, and in a flash, became a total know-it-all on the history of the Soviet revolution.

The same thing happened with the Gaullists. Because of his discretion and his nice smile, the father got himself enrolled in the party of Charles de Gaulle by a school principal who also needed a fine suit. The end result? Depending on which orders came in, he'd become either a Gaullist or a communist, especially because he was crazy enough to agree with every idea that was expressed in his presence. He'd always remark, "Once you've said that, you've said it all."

It was his way of showing neutrality, but everyone else just thought he was agreeing with them. And I can guarantee that he never added another word. Not a "You're so right," or a "Well, there I tend to disagree."

Only that expression: "Once you've said that, you've said it all," which, of course, is just a way to say nothing at all.

He also knew how to keep his mouth shut if by chance the communist and the Gaullist got into an argument in front of him, because it sometimes happened that they both showed up around the same time for a fitting. Who knows why he never thought to give them appointments at different times. He just said, "Come by when you can."

So, of course, they'd have at it in his workshop of just about two square meters. And in the middle of all those different-colored spools of thread rattling around on the floor, the piles of cloth, catalogs, tape measures, needles—and the mice those mounds of paper and cloth had attracted—the two opponents always battled it out, insulting each other. The father watched out for himself by keeping his mouth full of straight pins.

Emmanuel became a kind of black robot, busying himself with his customers, his chest covered in pins, his mouth full of them. The two men were so involved in their squabbling, it didn't even occur to them to ask his opinion. In any case, his mouth was sealed on those occasions, and all he could manage was an occasional "Mmmm," which could mean anything.

※

Oh, oh! I see a few other ghosts milling about. My, they're growing impatient, but I can't *not* talk about this aspect of his character. The child is still young, and we can't allow her to wait for explanations from a father who never had an opinion of his own in the first place.

What could he possibly teach her?

He's probably already messed his pants with all the events going on, and it's not like he'd be the one to ask questions about a teacher who's gone missing. I even wonder how upset he'd be if someone told him one of his kids had been wounded during the rioting. Maybe he'd say, "What in hell was he doing there?"

As if the fact of sidling into an alley and getting yourself beat up by a band of crazed soldiers proves how wrong you were to walk, just to walk, to get home from school or to run an errand for your mother—a simple everyday activity turned catastrophic.

I've only ever thought of the child's father as a castrated rooster, as cowardly as a fart in the wind, a *conseiller-j'applaude*, agreeing with everyone—except (I'd almost forgotten this) when he screams that old refrain, the one we were taught a long time ago, the one we repeat without a second thought: "You need a whip to get those blacks moving!"

His thunderous voice could be heard even in the farthest corners of our neighborhood's courtyards, especially when he went after his children, usually the boys—because his daughters were princesses and untouchable, at least most of the time. And we heard that voice too when he went after his wife; then it seemed to occupy the entire street, becoming a kind of sheet that swelled in the wind, growing bigger, flying horizontally, and projecting its shadow on the ground. But after having really strutted its stuff—pecs, tummy, ass—a sheet in the wind will suddenly lose its volume and hang limply from a clothesline. Now it's big in front, now it's big in back, but now—*flop!*—the wind stops, and it falls flat, lifeless, all dried up.

Well, Sauveur Emmanuel is just like that sheet when his wife gets angry. She'd finally snap and jump on him or throw a jug of wine in his face. He never expected it, and from the black fellow he was, he'd turn gray and trembling, calling out for help or stuttering, "*Mé ka i rivé'y?*" And again, "But what's got into her?"

Then his voice would shrink to a mere hesitation, stammering accompanied by a little smile, a smile seeking forgiveness. "Come on, you know my yelling doesn't mean anything!"

After that tiny embarrassed smile, he'd shrug his shoulders and flee, while the mother's voice would grow louder and faster, penetrating our streets, our little homes, even our bedrooms like a strong draft—while we kept prudently silent.

Frankly, when I say he's a coward, I know I'm judging him too harshly. Of course he's not the only person like that; his whole family is careful not to take too many risks. They take some, just what's necessary to move up in the world, slipping in here and there, moving if possible without a hitch from one rung of the ladder to the next. And all of this carefully, slowly—but sometimes they explode without warning, as if to loosen the reins of their silent rage.

Really, when I think about it, this cowardice disguising itself as excessive caution is pretty much the norm for the entire neighborhood. Sometimes even the roosters won't crow. They're being prudent, as if their singing might reveal an opinion.

You might say I'm exaggerating, but I swear it's true. All a politician has to do is show up, and the chickens kneel while the bull turns into a field mouse. The men's voices, usually heard loudly complaining about the mayor, turn to whispers. Their heads incline, as if begging for something. They stammer; they laugh with the mayor or his lackeys; they offer him a shot of rum and charge it to the account they'll have to pay later with money they aren't earning. A total transformation.

I mean, when I think about it—or think about it again—why should I use the word "cowardly"? What makes me think they aren't courageous? If you really dig into this story, you'll see that everyone has a hell of a burden to carry, just with getting up in the morning and continuing to live their lives, with customers who don't pay, salaries that never come in. There are so many songs about it; we can't pretend it's only a matter of complaining. And those hordes of children tumbling out of their wives' bellies like red ants streaming out of a discarded loaf of bread during Lent, those debts accumulating in little shops—and that impression of never quite getting on top of things, that blacks are damned for all eternity, from century to century.

They have to be clever, tricky, and act like a fox—but all that leaves scars on the spirit. You can't forget the other side of the coin: hating yourself for what you've become, for constantly questioning your life. You can end up detesting yourself, imagining what others think of you, and then rebelling, violently. You demand respect by brandishing a knife, consideration by carrying a revolver. You take revenge for slights you've only invented in your mind.

Some are satisfied, not by killing anybody, but by taking on another personality, by putting on a courageous and valiant face that shrinks any imaginary adversary. For example, when the child's father tells his own story, he becomes gutsy and daring. He's always the one speaking the loudest, while his enemies sound like weaklings, with voices he'd prefer not to have, to never have, so as to not sound pathetic.

How he rants and raves: "By God, I tell you, if I'd really let myself go . . . If only I'd had the authority . . . If even for a moment . . . If only God had given me the strength . . . Oh, what I would have done . . . You can't even imagine what I'm capable of doing."

I think I imitate him pretty well. Yeah, that's the child's father, all right. The father she's waiting for in the courtyard, while trying to fend off her fears.

THE SECOND FIGURE: *L'ÉTÉ*

1.

We call forth *l'été*! Let the dance begin!
Take your places; everyone to your place!
Escort the queen to the door!
Accept her salutations!
And let *ma-commère* prepare his entrance; his turn is next.
His is the violin's role.
The accordion player gives way to the violinist, and the
dancers quiet down!
They say the violin's too sad? What are they saying? Do
they imagine we've invited them to an orgy, a *voyé monté*?
My God, pay attention to the caller! You know nothing
at all about this quadrille, Émilienne's.
We, the chorus of brothers and sisters, know the little
one like no one else, and for once we're listening carefully to her needs.
Better than any of us, our Émilienne hears what the
silence says. The music of the last three days will
emerge from the strange universe she's summoned.
We're looking at Thursday, and so much has happened
on Thursday! So please, a little patience.
My friends, the night must unfold slowly until dawn slips
in. Our quadrille will evolve according to the musicians
who appear.
Let us wager that our Émilienne will invite into the
courtyard soloists whose virtuosity, when they play their
part in this story, is still out of our ken.

And let us indulge her decision to stay put, for hours on end, without moving, without a fuss, without making a scene—all the while feeling the air chill and the night settle in, waiting for voracious shadows to cover the country and render ever more invisible what we can hardly see, even now.

2.

Did somebody mention me? Hilaire?

Well, I'm asking because I thought I heard somebody bring up "the guy who hanged himself in his cottage."

Unless they called me "that faggot."

Excuse me for asking, but here I am.

And before I start, I have a message for you from the man who fell off the roof of city hall. Old Élie.

He asked me to tell you that he's not coming tonight. He won't even try. Nope, he's refusing to stick his nose in whatever's happening in this little corner of the universe. He's not in very good shape, and he's mad because his drinking buddies always teased him about how rum was such a great preservative. They used to say that he'd probably take a real long time to rot, seeing as how he put down so many pints—what am I saying, *barrels*—of rum. Shit, he wasn't thinking of that when he was downing all that booze with his pals. Regardless, watching himself disappear in puddles on the ground, well, that just makes him hopping mad, as red as a toad in heat. His innards being pressed out of him like liquid from a blood sausage, and his head swelling and swelling so much he's gonna end up looking like a giant pumpkin sitting in a muddy pool.

But boy, did he drink a ton of rum in Petit Curé's corner store. "Little Priest," that's the nickname we gave the grocer who drank all the time but ran his shop just fine somehow—and he never missed a morning mass. Okay, I know we're not here to listen to old war stories from the neighborhood, but all the same . . . So, how is this organized anyway? Everybody speaks in turn? You join in and you talk about what's bothering you, about your shitty life? I'm asking because that old lady who took the floor a minute ago, she barely touched on what's really bothering the little kid.

Just where is her schoolteacher?

3.

Thursday morning, May 25, 1967. I still can't understand why you didn't come home.

Mama doesn't answer when I wake up and ask, "Did Papa leave already?"

Emmy's preparing some homemade chocolate for us. She calls me over and says, "Stop asking where Papa is like that!" She doesn't yell. Instead she tries to speak softly, but she's creasing her forehead. So I move away.

I shrug and I hear her yell, "Émilienne!" I apologize right away.

You don't shrug when an older person speaks to you. You never respond to your elders, "Leave me alone!" You never suck your teeth, "*Tchluup.*" You never ever yell, "Oh boy!" as if the sky were falling. I know all her commandments, and it isn't worth having to recite them on my knees in the courtyard.

So, "I'm sorry, Emmy."

For a day off, today sure is starting off on the wrong foot.

Emmy is usually so sweet to me, and on Thursdays we do a lot of things together. But this Thursday everybody seems to be in a bad mood.

I help Emmy prepare some lemon zest for the cacao and cinnamon, but I wonder what's really going on.

We set the table in the courtyard, put out our breakfast bowls, and we all sit down: Mama, Émérite, our oldest sister, Emmy, Émelie, Émilie, Emmanuel, Émilio, Emmett, Émile, and Émilienne.

I understand why Mama can't remember all our names in one go. She always says the idea of giving all the children nearly the same first name as yours was crazy. Her own name is Emma, almost a copy! Mama says the whole gaggle tires her out. (You say we're more like a pod of dolphins.) But on Thursdays, when we're all present, we're really a great family, especially when you join us, Papa—even if you don't like chocolate.

After breakfast, I remember the report card in my book bag. With Émile sticking his nose in everything, I have to hide it somewhere. If he opens my book bag— supposedly to borrow my protractor, my T square, or my compass because he's always losing his own things— he won't hesitate to take a peek at my report card. And then there'll be "hell to pay." (That's an expression you really like Papa. You always say, "There's sure to be hell to pay." And then you laugh.)

So I wrap my report card in a plastic bag from the grocery store and hide it behind the green metal filing cabinet where you keep your bills and your workers' papers. It's a very heavy piece of furniture, and nobody bothers to move it to do the housework. That's what I tell myself. There's always a bunch of things that fall behind the furniture, but nobody ever has the energy to push aside a gigantic cabinet to clean up whatever is sleeping in the dust.

I'm so relieved that Mama signed my report card, I want to keep us from ever talking about it again. Please, let her not think about it!

And no one does ask to look at my grades. So eventually even I stop thinking about it and start my assigned chores.

On Thursdays, I'm supposed to clean the blue bathroom. I really like the blue bathroom. I don't know why I'm supposed to clean it because nobody ever uses it, but when I go up there, it's true it's always a little dirty. It's because those lizards who cling to the ceiling, those *mabouyas*, like to poop on everything.

The blue bathroom is brand new and still smells like fresh cement. I rub the flawless sink, I scour the shower, I wash the floor with a lot of water. I create a bunch of suds and slide across the tiles. When I've rinsed and dried everything, I like to stand in front of the mirror Mama installed. I don't know why.

But this Thursday I don't have time to plant myself in front of the mirror and repeat my "favorite mantra," as Emmy likes to say: "I have no name. I have no face."

Mama is calling me. Marlyse is downstairs in the courtyard waiting for me.

4.

What's happened to the schoolteacher?

We're in agreement, right? That's the theme of our meeting? At least that's what I've understood. Me, Hilaire. But instead of answering this seemingly innocent question, we've been skirting the issue; we recount our lives or we evoke happy memories. It's normal because, frankly, the mystery of the missing schoolteacher calls for a strong tremolo. In this I agree with the quadrille callers; Nono's accordion can't tell the tale right. I'm telling you, it's real tragic business, and for that we need a violin.

Unless we think the schoolteacher has found something better.

We could pretend she's accepted a more satisfying job than teaching a bunch of little girls whose legs are chalky and hair is messy after only an hour of class, kids who sweat like a pan of chestnuts over an open fire, kids who naturally smell of sour onion.

Maybe the administration offered her the chance to join the Normal School, the exclusive training institute destined for the new teaching elite, located in the cool heights of Morne Miquel. A replacement for her position as a grammar school teacher in that not very nice school by the sea smelling of piss and surf, where it's hard to talk over the noise of the cars passing by and the buses that block the crosswalks and rev their engines.

Maybe she was dreaming of leaving that establishment, where it's impossible to teach the nation's history with the merchant ladies on the quays raucously advertising their freshly caught fish—with the smell of diesel fuel from the ship *Île d'émeraude*, which ferries people back and forth from Marie-Galante, in the air. And let's hope that ship doesn't catch fire like the *Oiseau des Îles*, which burned up in the harbor last summer.

What a thing to happen, what a show! Fuel had leaked out of the engine, and that black, shiny grease was just waiting for a little spark to burst into flames. The chickens and rabbits kept in cages in the back of the ship were roasted and the potatoes were grilled in big jute sacks piled up on the bridge. Fire danced across the top of the oil right up to the port, and the firefighters had no idea how to handle any of it: how to put out the fire, how to evacuate the passengers, how to fish out the drowning—while seabirds laughed hysterically, looking on from the horizon, playing at being spectators.

We might be surprised to learn that all the teacher's loving kindness, all that dancing around about personal revolution, all that sappy poetry about discovering one's identity, all that wasn't enough to keep her from grasping at a new carrot.

What a stinking idea! What a lying explanation! Just the ranting of a nobody.

I know this kind of talk would have gotten me killed, no questions asked, if I weren't already rotting in my soapbox, my secondhand coffin that's already falling apart—which is why I prefer to think of myself as a hanged man dressed in off-white, wearing a trilby.

5.

I'm surprised Mama doesn't send Marlyse away, telling her that "Émilienne has things to do."

Everybody has to finish their chores on Thursdays, not spend hours gabbing on the sidewalk or in the courtyard. That's what I've always understood. And then, after our showers, we have Thursday morning dictation. And Marlyse knows that too!

I'd finished washing the bathroom a while ago, but I wanted to stay up there and daydream. The others don't pay attention to me when they don't see me.

"Are you busy?"

"No, it's okay. What's up?"

"I've been thinking about our teacher. Do you think she'll be back tomorrow?"

"She said she would."

Marlyse doesn't seem to believe it, so I try to reassure her. "Of course she'll be back. She said she'd leave at the end of the month."

Her visit really has me surprised. Marlyse rarely comes to my house because her parents are Jehovah's Witnesses; they don't like her to spend time with "worldly" people. Marlyse has already explained that the *world* is anybody who isn't a Jehovah's Witness; it's hell and Beelzebub. I think those are pretty funny names: Beelzebub, Jehovah. Marlyse can't tell me what language they come from, but we don't talk a lot about that stuff when we're together. We'd rather laugh.

Marlyse hands me a little bag. "Take it, it's my table runner. We don't do that, Mother's Day, I mean. I finished it last night while everybody was sleeping. But I can't give it to my mama. If you want, give it to yours." She smiles at me.

I hid my report card and she hid her table runner.

I watch her walk away.

And then I realize that the men who usually work on our house haven't shown up. I wonder if they didn't come because you've disappeared.

Maybe you'll never come back and we'll spend the rest of our lives in an unfinished house; the wooden ladder that leads to the third floor will always stay put because there'll never be a third floor.

I'm used to the workers. I normally see them when I go up to clean my bathroom. That is, I *hear* them. They pass each other pails full of concrete on a rope pulley. They make the concrete by mixing cement, sand, pebbles, and water in that machine, your big Sambron, turning and turning on the sidewalk, making a lot of noise.

"When are they going to stop that machine? It's wearing me out." Mama can't stand the dust from the cement, the piles of sand and pebbles in the courtyard, the sand the workers track all over, the huge barrel they have to fill with water all the time.

"Madame Emmanuel, can we hook up the hose?" Liters and liters of water sometimes spill all over the place when they're not paying attention, and this always sets Mama off. She yells, "Guy-Albert, does your father work for the water plant?"

"Beg your pardon, Madame Emmanuel."

I hear them tell all kinds of stories. They laugh. They make fun of each other. It's like that all the time, I mean every Thursday, that is, when they come. But this Thursday, they're not here. It feels like they've deserted us.

The sand sieve, I think it's called a sifter, is still on top of the wheelbarrow, full of sand. For once, Émile and I aren't wheeling around and pushing each other. The silent work site gives me the creeps; I don't feel so good.

Mama says, "No dictation today. I have too much work to do."

That doesn't make sense. We're all here on Thursday to help her out, so she has less to do. I think she's just really angry.

Émile couldn't be happier. He hates dictation. He runs off to La Place de la Victoire. He's probably scared Mama will send us to do math problems with Mademoiselle Potrizel, the neighbor who runs the day care school Mama sends us to for tutoring when she's had enough.

He leaves in a flash!

Emmy tries to catch him. "Where do you think you're going? To play drums? Don't you have homework?"

He doesn't answer. He's already far away. She's the only one who tries to control him. Mama has given up.

I run to the sidewalk to see where he's heading and catch sight of him as he turns the corner on rue Vatable. It's clear he's going to La Place.

People are waiting for the bus in front of our house. I hear them say nobody has seen Léogane's green buses. That's true, I haven't seen Léogane or Mauril today.

I don't have permission to speak to Mauril—the one who helps the market ladies load their baskets on the roof of the bus—nor to the drivers. They're adults and I must respect them, Mama says, just like they must respect me. Mauril, whose voice cracks, waves to me when he sees me. Mama doesn't like that. No one will ever see Mama engaged in conversation with bus drivers or the owners of bus lines.

I love Léogane's green buses. The name is painted in red on the two doors and on the back, some letters filled in, others just outlined, and red, yellow, and white hibiscus flowers are painted around them. It looks like the name is sleeping in a field of flowers, in the bed of the letter L, with the lower part stretching farther and farther out . . . But nobody knows why the Léogane buses haven't left the garage today.

6.

When people think about me, they see a hanged man.

Mademoiselle Pansy hanged himself. Man, what those two sisters must have been feeling in the back bedroom, the one over there, to the right of Émilienne's little bench. The elder sisters' bedroom. I'd love to look in and watch them sleep, those two girls who ran to my house to watch me dangling at the end of a rope. They didn't imagine they'd have nightmares and have to wake up their father in the middle of the night—what a grand idea for him to install a bell in his princesses' bedroom. They cried that the *ma-commère*—that's me—had just grabbed their feet.

Where the hell does that story come from, that the dead pull on your feet? Don't we have enough to do? With all the work you're saddled with when you get to the other side! To start, you're forced to go over every last detail of your life, live it all over again in your mind to understand how one thing led to another. We basically continue the work that starts when we turn sixty. We take apart the seams; we unroll the balls of yarn. Other people think we're just repeating ourselves, rehashing and rambling, but the truth is, nature doesn't give us a choice. It's as though everything is hardwired in our genes; you have to travel back in time.

It starts out real softly with "I remember, I remember . . ."

It's no wonder that phrase—in all the languages I know and even those I haven't mastered—serves as an anchor for so many different kinds of books, novels, and poems: *Je me souviens, Me acuerdo, An ka sonjé* or *Mi ricordo, Amarcord, Ich erinnere mich.*

What are we trying to find out by remembering?

Even the little one. She's barely nine years old, and I know she's going to regale us with all the memories she's accumulated of her teacher in just one single year. And she'll go back farther, farther, and farther, back to the first years when she was only a baby.

But let's not panic! I'm not trying to shut anyone up! That'd be impossible anyway; human beings have to talk. There's nothing to be done about it. They just won't shut up. But all the same, what I love in that child's worrying is the feeling of having lost a world that was just beginning to blossom in front of her, different from everything else she's seen till now. At least that's what I'm able to understand.

That schoolteacher represented her future. She suggested new ways of living, how to confront what her country is, its history, a way of shaking up her perceptions.

I would've liked for somebody along the way to have opened a door for me and shown me a future where all this harassment, all this name-calling—pansy, faggot, fairy, and queer—could actually end.

I would've liked to have had another option besides

stringing that noose around my neck and being hoisted up off the ground with one quick jerk, leaving behind the singular and unforgettable image of shit erupting from my body and soiling what was left of me.

I would've really appreciated being spared an entire life of depression and loneliness.

7.

Around eleven o'clock, I'm told to pick out the pebbles in the dried lentils. While I do this, I go over what's happened the last few days in my head.

Wednesday: my teacher tells us she's probably going to have to leave. My father doesn't come home.

Thursday: the workers don't show up. The Léogane buses don't park in their usual place, and Marlyse lies to her mother so she can come over and worry with me about our teacher.

With these lentils from Madame Plaucoste, I have loads of time to sift through different versions. There are tons of stones to remove.

I grumble, "Madame Plaucoste is nice enough, but these lentils are really awful! There are more pebbles than lentils."

"We're not going to stop doing business with her. She's our friend, our good neighbor," Mama says.

We'll only go elsewhere when she doesn't have what we need and tells us to try the competition: "See if Ninita has it!"

I'm wearing out my eyes looking for pebbles (it's Mama who's always wearing out her eyes sifting through rice, lentils, and even red beans), when all of a sudden Émile reappears, running. "Mama, guess what?"

"Where were you?" She's so formal, he's caught up short.

He left without permission. If he can't manage to think up an excuse, he'll spend the whole day in the courtyard in his underpants because Mama will soak all his other clothes to keep him from going out again.

"You said we weren't going to have dictation, so I went over to Gustarimac's to do math." Gustarimac is his best friend, the only thing he talks about.

Mama must not feel like wasting energy because neither Gustarimac nor my brother is known for his skills at math. She leaves him alone and goes off to fry fish.

Émile doesn't know who to share the big news with, especially news no one wants to hear, so he sits down next to me, on the bench by the table. He starts to put his hands in the lentils, mixing the good lentils with the pebbles I'd already found and put to the side.

"Are you doing that on purpose?"

"I saw your favorite teacher's husband."

I don't know Madame Ladal's husband, so why would he? "You always know more than anybody else. How'd you know it was her husband?"

"They live in the same house and they walk side by side on the street. Who do you think it is, her father?"

"So just where did you see him?"

Émile tells me he wasn't at Gustarimac's. I of course already knew that. They were together, but out in the street. That's what those two like to do: hang out in the streets, borrow bikes, and go to places Mama can't even imagine, like Poucette, where they go swimming in the creek. I don't even know where Poucette is. I hear about it, but as far as I'm concerned, it's a non-place, as if Émile invented it just to make me jealous.

"Near the big post office. Rue Gambetta."

"What's there?"

"People screaming in front of the police station."

"And my teacher's there?"

"I told you—her husband!"

He can't tell me why people are gathered in front of the police station. He didn't really understand what was happening, and then Éric, Emmy's fiancé—well, really her gentleman caller, who we call "orangutan" because he's so hairy—stepped out of the crowd. He made straight for Émile and ordered him to go home.

"I almost told that guy off, but I felt sorry for him."

Papa, I think he was scared that Éric would tell you that he'd seen him in his shorts and bare feet in downtown Pointe-à-Pitre. He always takes his shoes off to run around town. Did you know that?

The part of the day I hate the most is just before lunch. I don't have enough to do then. I can't go out because we're going to eat soon, and I can't read because somebody always finds a little job, something really insignificant, for me to do.

I try to finish my table runner. But to do this without Mama seeing, I hide in the armoire in the bedroom.

Once there, I know I'll be left alone for a little while. But I have to leave the door ajar so I don't suffocate, and I need a little light.

I'm stuffed between dresses and shoes. Every dress has a different smell; some of them smell a little like sweat. Mama tells us we shouldn't wash our clothes too much or they'll lose their color. We hang our dresses outdoors, in the wind, to air them out, but when they're back in the closet, it seems like all the odors come back, especially the underarm ones.

I don't care. The smell from the shoes doesn't bother me either. I push everything towards the back of the armoire, even the dresses, and that gives me a nice little space.

I try not to make any noise, because if I do, one of my brothers will guess I'm hiding in the closet and lock me in.

I'm working on my plastic corks when Emmy and Émelie come into the bedroom to talk. They don't realize I'm in the armoire. They probably think I'm in front of the mirror in the blue bathroom. I can hear everything they say.

"I wonder if the 'patriarch' is coming back."

"It's not the first time he hasn't come home."

"But this time Éric says it's serious."

"What's serious?"

"The strike. Didn't you notice that the workers didn't come this morning?"

"You think they went after Papa?"

"Don't you remember the one who came into the salon and threatened him?"

"That's all been worked out."

"Does it ever really get worked out?"

"I think Papa slept at his sisters' place and he's at some work site now."

"But the work sites are all blocked. Éric told me there'd be work stoppages everywhere."

"Éric this and Éric that. Are you going to marry him or what?"

"I just want to get out of this house."

"At any cost? The guy's a skirt chaser."

"Can you prove it? No, right? So shut up!"

Papa, everybody in the family is wondering about you. Especially your daughters.

I know that Mama, too, is asking what's so important that you haven't come home, even if she's still running the show, like any other day.

She serves us lunch—nine children around the table—then asks Émilie to take care of the dishes and goes off to rest.

Afterwards, I stretch out next to her, and she asks, "What will we have to eat tonight?"

She always asks that question right after our noon meal. What will we have to eat tonight? Sometimes she doesn't even need to ask it. I ask before she does. We lie down side by side and I say, "What will we have to eat tonight?"

She laughs. I like to see her laugh.

But this time, she isn't joking. She asks the usual question, but she's thinking about something else. I can see in her eyes that she's far, far, far away, and she murmurs, "What a strange day . . . So very strange."

And then she looks at me, ruffles my hair, and whispers, "You're lucky to still be a child, my little fox. Take advantage of it. The best times in life are when you're a child or in the army . . . youth . . ."

I want to take advantage of the moment by asking her why we aren't going to look for you, wherever you are. But I remember Emmy forbade me to ask that question. ("Stop asking where Papa is . . .")

So I ask something else, "Why do I have to take catechism from Madame Jabol? My teacher also gives catechism lessons."

"You know, Madame Ladal is a devout Christian, but her husband's a communist. It doesn't look good." She adds, "Your father doesn't know this, but I have nothing against communists. In fact, I always vote for them."

I don't understand why she's telling me this and why, if she votes communist, she doesn't want me to take catechism from Madame Ladal. But I don't say anything. I understand that in these matters you're the one who decides, Papa.

8.

It was plenty hard being a pansy in this world. A real trial, believe me.

Having a big mouth and being arrogant didn't help at all either. You had to be strong, act as though nothing could get to you. That would do it. But it was like being crucified. Everything was a crucifixion: the way people looked at you, the way you *thought* they looked at you, the questions on their lips, the hesitant glances.

"Tell me it's not what I think it is!"

Some of them would start shaking uncontrollably from disgust. You know how some panic—there's no other word for it—when they come face to face with a queer. Maybe they panic because, when you get down to it, they're actually attracted. It's tempting to let your-self plunge into the realm of the forbidden, to give in to the tiny suggestion that's been sleeping in your gut. Even me, who always knew I wanted to be with men, I've been shaken up by a woman who propositioned me, naively offering herself up, not getting who I was. All it takes is a smell, the softness of skin, a moment of aban-don where you're, you know, near another person and your blood starts to rage; you hear their body calling you and your legs get weak—all of that, you know. So of course you feel like letting yourself go because it's been too long, really too long since you had someone show you a little tenderness, someone to put your arms around. It's like that: nobody to put your arms around, or hold next to you, so you feel your body actually exists, to sense your blood running through your veins, to know you're really alive, still kicking.

I'm not lying when I say it was difficult for me, but I never gave in. I always waited for the man who was gonna share my life to show up.

How I've been going on! When you're human, you just can't stop yourself from telling your own story. I've already sidestepped the topic at hand to launch into an analysis of my own little life, even when nobody gives a shit, really not a shit! Why isn't anybody stopping me? Why isn't the kid herself saying, "Listen, Mademoiselle Pansy, you're nice and all, but tonight I'm waiting for my father and what he has to say about why my teacher disappeared. If you don't have anything to share to help us out, just shut up!"

But there she is, sitting like a good little girl on her bench, a little stiff, yeah, as tight as a soul singer's shirt. Even I, passed over to the other side as I am, look more alive than she does. I bet she's tense like that because she's afraid of wild animals and insects. And boy do I understand that. I won't treat you to the meltdowns I've had when I've seen those battalions of cockroaches all exiting my plumbing at once. And the way their feet scrape the walls and the wood floors . . . Maybe we should talk about something else.

So just what important information can I share tonight?

For one thing, you should know that being a homosexual in this country forces you to suffer the mysteries of snitching, without being a participant.

I mean as a victim, of course.

You learn pretty quick how to recognize the signs in how others look and act. Having been a schoolteacher myself, I bet I can guide the kid to the man or woman, and I think it probably was a woman, who informed on her teacher and delivered her to the authorities.

My guess is it started with a forbidden book. Of course there are forbidden books! Just because Madame Ladal passed on her passion for reading, you shouldn't think everybody shared her devotion, and especially not for every book.

Literature. Nobody has sniffed around that question yet! How important it is, what its role might be, how dangerous it can feel. The few poems her students learned were already a little subversive, not to mention how she taught African authors and stories when they were just supposed to stick with "Little Red Riding Hood," "Snow White and the Seven Dwarves," and "Monsieur Seguin's Goat." Madame Ladal marched to the beat of her own drum, that's for sure, not like those other teachers.

And I heard she had the odd tendency of explaining to her students the bigger meaning behind the stories of Ti-Jean, Brer Rabbit, and Big Zamba, relating all their adventures to the organization of plantation society. Can you imagine: speaking about the struggles between workers and bosses, slaves and plantation owners, when reading a simple folktale. Well, I doubt that contributed to her colleagues liking her any, or made the school principal willing to stick her neck out.

9.

As I'm preparing to leave for catechism, Mama is singing Gluck: "*J'ai perdu mon Eurydice. Rien n'égale mon malheur.*" (I can't stand it when she sings that!) "*Quelle souffrance! Quel tourment déchirent mon coeur!*"

She's already preparing the vegetables for our soup tonight. She's cutting up squash, carrots, and celery into smaller and smaller cubes, and the smaller the cubes, the sadder she sings. She sounds so sad I almost feel like staying to comfort her. But I have to go do something I can't tell her about. "Mama, I'm leaving."

"Going where? Oh yes, to catechism. Are your sisters walking with you? Émilie!"

"It's not necessary, Mama. It's right next door. I always go by myself."

"But today, oh today . . . All right, go ahead."

I don't want anyone to go with me because I'm planning to stop by my teacher's house to ask if she'll be back at school tomorrow.

Madame Jabol won't see me in class today. That's my idea when I leave the house. Madame Jabol can just wait.

I pass by her door pretty proud of myself. The other children are reciting their catechism. Luckily the shades are drawn because of the sun, so no one sees me stroll by.

I walk down rue Commandant Mortenol, cross rue

Alexandre Isaac, and reach La Place de la Victoire, where I find myself in front of my teacher's house.

All the doors are closed. All the shutters too. All of them.

So, she's already left? She didn't even teach catechism today? She stopped everything? She's really disappeared?

I don't know what to do. I can't tell anybody at home that my teacher's doors are shut, that she's abandoned everything, left it all behind. They'll ask me how I know.

Nobody's at La Place; the gates of the government offices are closed, so the subprefecture looks deserted; my school's empty. It looks like everyone has left town.

So I walk back to Madame Jabol's.

※

After catechism, Annie stops to talk to me.

She's not really my friend; she's my rival. She does everything she can to steal first place from me, and I have to put up with her sitting next to me because of the teacher's funny idea: that whoever is in first place always sits next to second place and so on.

Sometimes I wish she were last so we wouldn't be at the same table.

But this month I'm in last place. Well, next to last, but it's basically the same thing. That means I have to sit at the desk at the back of the class, near the window facing the street. I bet Madame Jabol would tell me, "God is punishing you because you hope for bad things to happen to your fellow men."

I was afraid Annie would run to tell her she was first

this month, since I was next to last, and that if I hadn't come to catechism it was probably because my parents were punishing me.

But Annie kept her big mouth shut.

Madame Jabol, who's also Émile's godmother, didn't say anything either and, oddly, Annie is waiting for me after class. "Can I walk home with you?"

"But you don't live in that direction."

"I don't feel like going home right away."

I don't answer and start to walk, in silence. We make our way side by side, still not talking. Finally, I have to say something; I need to talk to someone too much.

"I think she's really gone."

"Our teacher?"

"Yeah, I walked by her house. Everything is closed up."

I'm not expecting at all what happens next. Annie starts to cry.

10.

Hilaire again. I'm not going to mince words about snitching.

Everybody betrays everybody else! It's essential to hold on to that at all costs. It's key to understanding this story and could also be a major factor behind the schoolteacher's disappearance. To better illustrate what I've just said, I'm going to tell you a couple of things about myself.

Now, I've already mentioned that people called me *ma-commère*. That's to say *man-woman*, a man dressed up in a feminine pronoun. Not to mention that the word *commère* means a terrible gossip.

It couldn't be any clearer than that, could it? But, you know, I didn't get stuck with that name until after hanging myself. The neighbors and all the others ran around the streets yelling, "*Ma-commère* has hanged himself!"

They were an army of black ants surging right up to my cottage: they pushed each other out of the way, giving free reign to their thoughts. Obviously the shit, the piss, the bizarre-looking head I had on top of my swollen neck, all this had people talking, their tongues wagging. But mine sure wasn't, by God, not that it was anything anybody should have seen. Already dead and gone to the ancestors, I wondered, with eyebrows raised, why the inhabitants of my neighborhood, of my town, were acting so vulgarly.

The news spread in the streets and everyone was invited to come gape at my miserable fate—abandoning any task at hand to greedily feed on the death of one poor soul, watching him swivel like a trapeze artist in his blue leotard, that shiny blue you see in circuses and carnivals. Except I didn't hold the rope between my teeth the way a trapeze artist might, as though it were a simple piece of cloth. My black and blue tongue lolled out of my mouth, my eyes rolled back in their sockets, and let's not forget the putrid stains on the darkened and dirty wood floor. Their curiosity appalled and offended me. How excessively gross and uncalled for! Didn't they realize they were just teaching their children to be coarse and brutish?

You have to think about how much this kind of experience forges character, especially a budding adolescent's. When you entertain a ten-year-old—and some children weren't even that old—by mocking how a man uses the most intimate part of his anatomy, when your ridicule is neither elegant nor elevated, when your dirty jokes about him make your whole family burst into sick laughter, you have to see that you're living like a beast.

And furthermore, if you're taught that it's natural to judge and denounce the "perversions" of such a person to the civil and religious authorities, you'll acquire a taste for snitching from very early on, in addition to a strong taste for crudeness.

11.

Annie's crying and I'm the one consoling her. Usually she's the tough, strong one. We've always been in the same class and she's always been mean. She must have changed.

I didn't notice it, but it seems like since we've had Madame Ladal as our teacher, Annie's stopped calling me an "aristocrat." She didn't once say that my papa, my mama, and all my family, myself included, must think we're pretty special. And she usually dragged out the "special."

So as I'm trying to comfort her, I think that maybe we've become friends without my realizing it—even if we still compete for first place.

I bring her home with me and even before I ask Mama if I can stay in the courtyard with my new friend, she answers, "Of course you may."

I whisper to Annie, "Don't mention my report card!"

She shakes her head. No, no. She won't say a word.

Annie and I don't do much; we look at the books we got as prizes. Annie's disappointed because she's already read two of them.

I'm luckier; I haven't read any of mine.

One is very old, as if our teacher received it when she was our age. It smells moldy. I don't really like the smell of mold, especially on books. I prefer the smell of new paper.

My very old book is called *Les Contes d'Amadou Koumba*. We'd never seen this collection of tales in our class's library. No one had ever taken it out before.

When we open it, Annie and I recognize a sentence our teacher made us copy in our notebooks at the end of each day: *The tree only grows by sinking its roots into Mother Earth.*

This makes us laugh, so we start to read the tales of Amadou Koumba out loud.

I read one story, Annie another, and from time to time we happen upon another phrase we've already copied into our notebooks: *Speaking too much is always a bad idea!*

I'll tell our teacher how we found those sayings, and I already feel real happy to be able to share this secret with Madame Ladal. But I'm not sure I'll ever see her again.

I see her locked doors; I see La Place as sad as the day they buried Pope John XXIII, when Mama cried while she listened to the big, slow voices singing on the radio.

And all of a sudden, I'm nervous. I say to Annie, "Let's not read it all right away! Besides, I have some things to do for Mama. You should probably go."

Mama, who's sewing in the courtyard, raises her head.

Annie is disappointed, and she asks, "You'll lend it to me, when you're finished, right?"

I say yes, but I already know I'll never lend this book to anybody, absolutely not. Never.

I'm angry, so angry I feel like stomping, stomping, stomping until my whole body aches.

Mama says very softly to Annie, "Well, you'll see each other tomorrow, won't you?"

Annie leaves and I go up to the blue bathroom.

I face my mirror. I finally face my mirror.

I'm angry, so angry and sad I'm about ready to pass out. But I don't want to cry. I can't stop repeating in my head, *You aren't going to cry, are you? You aren't going to cry!*

I try to calm down, but I can't. Every time I'm this angry, my whole body itches. I have to hold myself back because if I don't, I'll scratch so hard I'll make myself bleed.

I say the two sentences that calm me down. I don't know how they came to me, but it does me good.

When I start breathing normally, I stop looking in the mirror. I sit on the floor of the balcony and think, as Mama often does, *Today I haven't had a single minute to myself.*

But I actually say it out loud, and I hear someone laugh. It's Mama. She came up and I didn't even hear her.

"Are you making fun of me?" she asks.

I answer, "Why do people disappear?"

She looks surprised. "Émilienne, you think too much for your age."

And so I tell her about my teacher, that her doors are closed and locked; I tell her that Emmy and Émilie think Papa isn't going to come home, that Émile saw people screaming in front of the police station, that maybe something terrible has happened and we don't know what it is, and that Emmy, on top of everything, is going to get married and leave me all alone. I tell her that

Annie cried because our teacher has disappeared, that Marlyse is worried. I didn't want to cry, but it just came out, and I yell at Mama, meanly, while crying, "You don't love Papa! That's why you're not looking for him!"

Mama tells me to get dressed. I don't understand what's going on. I was waiting for her to strike me and make me get on my knees. The last time I got mad at her, I told her she wasn't my mama, because if she were my mama she'd never hit me. I also said I must be a child she found in the garbage. That's what she says sometimes when she feels like joking, but I took it seriously. I yelled real loud at Mama and she made me kneel in the courtyard. Do you remember, Papa?

That day, you didn't tell me to get up. Usually you don't like it when I'm forced to kneel but you simply shook your head. "So just like that your mother isn't your mother? You really are an extraordinary child!"

This time I know what I said hurt her, but she isn't getting angry. "Go get dressed!"

When I walk down to the girls' bedroom, everybody watches me pass by: Émérite, Émilie, Émilio, Émile. Emmett, who'd been playing the piano, stops to look at me. Émelie whispers, "You're crazy, little girl!"

Emmy isn't there to defend me, not that I know she would. Emmanuel, the most timid of all of us, has disappeared. He must be watching things from a distance.

Mama says, "Put your best shoes on!"

I pick out my red dress with the blue flowers and my red patent-leather shoes, the ones with a little strap that buttons over my ankle.

I think maybe Mama is going to abandon me or give

me back to the person who really is my mother, and I'm afraid. But I obey.

She gets dressed too. She hadn't gone out once all day and had been wearing an old housedress. She washes her arms and face and then slips on her sleeveless dress, the striped one. She grabs a scarf, a kind of beige mantilla. Maybe she's going to take me to church so that I can ask forgiveness for what I've said.

But when we leave, we take a very different route than the one that goes to church.

We walk down boulevard Hanne; we pass in front of Amie Lou's house, the person who gives coconut sweets to Emmett so he'll play for her.

Some people are buying blood sausage from a lady seated on a little stool in front of a bucket shining in the streetlights. That lady is there every evening, but Mama never buys *boudin* from her because she's dirty. Anyway, we're not out for a walk to buy blood sausage.

It's already getting dark. I've never gone so far in this direction, and never in the evening.

All my brothers and sisters have stayed home and Mama is taking me somewhere, I don't know where. And I'm afraid because she's squeezing my hand hard and not saying a word.

12.

"It's amazing how a clean sheet can mask a dirty mattress."

How many times have I heard that, ringing out like a death knell from the mouth of the person who first snitched on me, Mademoiselle Potrizel?

She boomed out that phrase every morning until my death, looking me straight in the eye, but I never looked away. Instead, I made do with greeting her respectfully by tipping my hat while she waved her hand in front of her face as if to chase away a foul smell. I no doubt smelled of lust—and God protect us from the Prince of Darkness and his evil deeds!

She was a childminder, a babysitter, that's what she was. She claimed to be teaching the neighborhood kids to read from books, books in which a mythical father smoked a pipe that never went out, unlike the pipe of our policeman neighbor who was devoted to the magazine *Détective*—which helped him solve any local mystery featuring naked women.

Mademoiselle Potrizel always had her eye on me. Often as I passed by, she'd give a little speech to whatever innocent kid happened to be at hand—not that they'd stay innocent for long! Sticking out her chin in my direction, she'd unleash her ritual phrase, "It's amazing how a clean sheet can mask a dirty mattress."

The child, thinking he was having a reading lesson,

always repeated the words "unclean," "sheet," and "dirty" while looking at me. He'd understood the essential: I was the unclean man in the dirty sheets.

Very dirty indeed, when the little angels' guardian stopped by the school I was teaching at and confronted the principal. She asked him point blank, "Are you aware that Hilaire, to whom you've entrusted our children, is doing business with the jeweler, and everybody knows it?" (That bitch only had access to the children of her neighbors, who had no idea what went on in her so-called school.)

An informant, a snitch, but incapable of coming right out with it. So she chose her words carefully to spark something in the principal's mind. "Doing business" referred to a Creole expression for lesbianism: Women who *font zafé*.

But maybe that's why, seeing as I was a man, the principal didn't get it. As far as the jeweler was concerned, everybody knew he liked men—but also that he sold jewelry he'd purchased on the cheap from women in dire straits. He profited from their financial difficulties, but that was all.

My principal must have thought I was involved in some black-market dealings for inexpensive jewelry, and—thank God—none of that seemed very important to him. He even remarked to me with a conspiratorial laugh, "Come on, Hilaire. You didn't even try to get me to buy something for my wife! You wouldn't let your principal miss a good bargain, would you? Your neighbor, Mademoiselle Potrizel, informed me of your little trafficking business. Try to be more discreet next time."

Our school was a vast market where the teachers,

all working second jobs, shamelessly sold every kind of thing under the sun: jewelry, perfume, yams, and christophenes, evangelical pamphlets like *Awake!*, tablecloths and clothing from Santo Domingo, shoes from Puerto Rico, soft candy from Saint Barts, lace from our own Vieux-Fort, cassavas from Capesterre, manioc flour and syrupy candies from Marie-Galante, hair gel and straightening creams from Miami—and, how could I forget, marvelous baby products such as Johnson's baby oil, which even I used, imported from the English islands surrounding us.

13.

Mama and I wind through a lot of little streets without sidewalks. The deeper we get into the neighborhood, the darker it gets.

There's no light at all, no street lamps—on our street there's a big light, and you say it keeps you from sleeping, Papa. But here there's nothing at all and the dark is making me scared, and besides, there's a funny smell.

Mama stops in front of a tiny pale-yellow house, also poorly lit. She knocks and a lady comes and opens the door. She jumps when she sees us. "*Ò-ò, Éma! Ka ki pasé?*"

They speak only in Creole. Mama answers that nobody's died or hurt, but they need to talk. I look hard at the lady and see she looks like you.

"Kiss your Aunt Lise; she's your father's sister."

Aunt Lise is still speaking Creole. "*É ki non a piti-lasa?*"

Mama answers, "This one's Émilienne."

"Oh yes, her father's little sweetheart! Kiss your auntie, darling."

Other ladies show up. They look like you too. Aunt Lise introduces me to Aunt Isabelle, Aunt Augustine, and Aunt Chimène.

They never come to our house, and we never go to theirs. I've never seen them, but I know you have lunch with them, dinner too, and you have a coffee with them the mornings you and Mama fight.

Papa's four sisters. Papa's four sisters. That's what I keep repeating in my head.

I don't really know why Mama brought me here. Maybe she's decided I love Papa so much that I should live with his sisters. That way I could see him every day, more often than at home.

But I don't want to leave Emmy and all the others, my house, the blue bathroom, Émile. I want to beg Mama to take me home. (Let's go, Mama!)

We sit down in the dining room around a huge shiny table, and I cross my arms, trying to act like a good little girl.

14.

Try to be more discreet.

The day after the babysitter's failed snitching attempt, I went over to the small costume shop near the entrance to the infamous alley sheltering her phony children's school. I bought a whole selection of half masks, full masks, flounced dresses, and false breasts from the old lady running the store. I dressed up as a bearded lady, ready to parade my stuff in front of the bogus teacher that Saturday morning. Did I mention she's a Seventh-Day Adventist—maybe even worse!

Try to be more discreet.

Saturday was a sacred day for her and her kind. As soon as Friday night rolled around, old Potrizel lowered her eyes, refused to acknowledge this sinful world on the road to damnation, and lost herself in loony conversations with a God who never asked for such a thing. She was supposed to emerge from her suffering for all of humanity's sins on Saturday night, at sunset and the end of Sabbath. Nevertheless, in order to show the world her faith, her plunge into sainthood was topped off by going to church in a lace dress, with her fanciest parasol and bright white shoes that made her feet look six meters long.

Try to be more discreet.

I knew when she was going to leave her house to play

out this holy carnival, so I accompanied her right up to the Adventist temple, more femme than her, with my falsies falling out of a stunning yellow dress, silky and formfitting, and in flesh-colored stockings. (Those pinkish stockings on my black legs had quite an effect!) And all the way along this crucifixion trail, I rattled a ton of bracelets, chains, and gold rings I'd worked at winning by feeding ten-centime coins, one at a time, into the bubble-gum machine in front of Madame Plaucoste's shop. Every piece of gum came with a little plastic egg that held a piece of jewelry, as precious as the juicy pink chiclet.

Try to be more discreet.

Our parade caught everybody's attention and provoked the hearty laughter of the streets. We heard the clucks of chickens and assembled turkeys, the cackles of hyenas and jackals, the grunting of squinty-eyed pigs—and the oinking rumblings provoked by a vulgar show. All the town's animal nature was on display.

I'd obviously hit the heights of discretion, and after that I wasn't going to hide anymore. The babysitter, the phony teacher, would know that her snitching had no power over me. At least that's what I thought. I assure you it's what I thought and what I sincerely wanted. I believed I'd crossed a threshold with my outlandish declaration, but I'd given myself too much credit that day and underestimated how dangerous Potrizel really was. She went crazy, running from one office to another, from the priest to the bishop, from the principal of the school to the director of the vice-rectory. Confusing homosexuality and pedophilia, she invented all kinds of stories about me, up until the moment I perfected my trapeze-artist act—without any kind of net, without a single hand held out to catch me.

Isn't it possible your schoolteacher made the same mistake?

Mama speaks first, "The child wants to know where her papa is."

Aunt Lise starts to explain, "What makes you think we would know?"

Aunt Augustine interrupts her sternly, "Don't start by lying, Lise. You'll make things even more complicated. Emma is Emmanuel's wife. She has the right to be worried. Emmanuel is our brother, not your husband. I'm tired of you acting like this! It's time to stop!"

Mama sighs.

I uncross my arms and start to monkey with my fingers. Aunt Augustine scares me; her eyes sink real deep in her head and she's skinny, too skinny. (She's taller than all the others, right, Papa?) Aunt Isabelle and Aunt Chimène are a little heavy, but not too much, not as much as Aunt Lise. At least that's how it seems to me.

Aunt Lise grumbles, "*Emmanuel vinn isidan bo maten-la.*"

(Is that true, Papa? You were here while we were waiting for you?)

Aunt Chimène gets up and comes back with some glasses: anisette liqueur for Mama and lemonade for me.

Aunt Augustine starts up again, "I'm telling you, Emma, we don't agree with everything Emmanuel does. He has his business and we don't interfere, but when our brother's in trouble, we support him. When he came over this morning, he was pretty worked up. He told us he was supposed to go to a meeting with all the other construction company owners, but he didn't agree with them. He told us not to wait for him for lunch or dinner because the meeting was sure to go on and on."

Mama says, "He hasn't come home since Wednesday, and this child, the one right here in front of you, thinks her Papa has abandoned us. Is that what's going on?"

All four of your sisters speak at the same time.

"Oh sweet pea, your father would never do such a thing! He loves you. He loves your Mama; he loves his children. You shouldn't think such a thing! Times are hard; that's all it is. Times are hard."

When we get up to leave, Aunt Lise says to me, "You'll have to come back to see us one of these days, okay?"

Everybody kisses me, and Aunt Isabelle even gives me a cinnamon stick covered in coconut.

16.

Well, just let me tell you—me, Queen Nono, as they're calling me now—that little girl, well she's just pulled off a miracle: getting her mother and her father's four sisters together, face to face.

Now let me speak!

Without knowing anything about the history of those women—why they don't speak to each other or go to each other's houses, or why the sisters don't even know their brother's youngest children—that child managed to get them to budge!

Should I tell you why these five women were enemies? Would you like me to explain it?

It's an old story that could've been resolved a long time ago if Sauveur Emmanuel himself hadn't benefited from widening the gulf between his wife and sisters. Divide and conquer, after all! Sauveur was the prince of two realms—the absolute ruler. But Sauveur Emmanuel was a prince without a treasury, and when I say "treasury," you should know the sisters always had one: from jewelry they sold, to small discreet business deals, to cakes prepared at home—in their wood cottage with the tin roof, a house the child only saw for the first time last night. They did piecework, poorly paid—some sewing and ironing, a couple of jobs as maids in an upwardly mobile household; a kind of trade set up by a country cousin whose vegetables they'd sell—but carefully saved the money they earned. You spoil your clientele, the money comes in regularly, and you take a percentage. Everybody lives like that, off of what comes in from a dozen small jobs, and since the state doesn't get a whiff of that money—and why on earth would you give the state some of what it can't even create and organize?—it's not taxed and gradually adds up.

But there's the prince, with his big ideas. So you have to help him out.

You see, it all came to a head because of the workshop.

He wanted to enlarge his tailoring business. The sisters were real happy with the idea: the business was clean, the clients were from the best families, they thought he could work at home. But that was the fly in the ointment: working at home.

They wanted him to set up shop in his house and stop paying rent for the workspace. They were ready to hand over some of their savings to create the biggest and most spectacular tailor shop in town.

They talked it over for days and days and even long into the night. He allowed himself to be convinced; he wasn't against the idea. "So how are we going to make this happen?"

It was Aunt Lise who had the idea about the salon and formal dining room. He just had to annul the lease on the workshop with his landlord and transport all his equipment into that large room in his house. "You have that great big room; there's enough space for the workshop and a little office in the back for taking orders and paying bills."

"But what about the furniture? Where do we put all that?"

"Well, you sell it!"

"But it was our wedding gift from Emma's mother. We can't do that."

"She has to choose. Does she want a future for her children or would she rather keep useless furniture? You always eat in the courtyard, and I've never seen you receive anybody in that room, which is always so perfect and clean—but what for? You can just buy something else when you have the money."

Stupid! Real stupid what Lise was saying, at least that's how I see it. You don't ask a woman to get rid of her family's wedding gift in order to make your own dreams come true. Maybe you can get your way for a while, but believe me, even if I've never been married, even if I didn't really have a mama, I know you have to pay attention to your partner. Especially when you have four sisters who're the apple of your eye and you'd never not listen to them for anything in the world. You have to be dumb not to understand that. But Lise insisted, and the other sisters agreed with her; so Sauveur Emmanuel tried to impose his will on Emma.

"Nothing doing. I'd rather see the workshop go up in smoke!"

She really said that! Sure did.

"I'd rather see your workshop go up in smoke than lose my mother's wedding present."

Of course I'm not going to recount everything that he said about her, about her mother, about past generations and generations to come, about the idiocy of little negresses who don't understand anything about coming up in the world! Of course he dared compare that pitiful descendant of a washerwoman to his blessed, adored, and understanding sisters. And so the small bubble of resentment already forming at their wedding burst. The sisters were forbidden to ever come to their home: "You will not bring my children to them either, and if one of them ever tries to greet me on the street, I'll tell her to go where Ti-Jean sent his stepmother!"

And that was that. Everybody knows where Ti-Jean sent his stepmother.

Boy oh boy! That was truly a declaration of war. He tried to retreat, to make her see his sisters didn't really have anything to do with the idea. He tried everything to make up for the mistake, which he willingly admitted to, but nothing doing. The sisters could never go to his home again. The children grew up without roots, but it wasn't going to kill them.

But today, what Émilienne pulled off—I tell you, you have to respect it!

Some children are like that; they're born and you ask, why did the family need a ninth kid, how are they going to feed it with all the others?

I've already told you—did I tell you?—I saw the little one's mama crying crocodile tears when she learned she was pregnant again. How she was raised, what her religion told her, she wasn't going to get rid of that child, and her husband would never have agreed in any case. No question about that! No, Emma didn't want that last one, like the three last ones before it. But every time they came, she loved them, even if she was a little harsh sometimes. She knew how to make them laugh, tell them stories about how bad she'd been when she was little, and give them those big wet kisses on their eyes.

Not so true for the bigger ones, but that's normal. Where we live, when a child grows up, you put some distance between herself and yourself. You yell and hit rather than give hugs. The big ones forget they'd ever been hugged, but they had their share of it, just like the others.

So, some children just surprise us. You wonder why they come and then one day you see what they're good for. Everyone has a place; everyone has a purpose.

When the child and her mama turned the corner, the conversation must have really taken off in the sisters' house. Lise probably got yelled at. You'd think that one was married to her brother! You had to hear her say, "*Emannuel frè an mwen! Ti-Manno an nou!*"

But "my little Mano" or not, if the sisters decide to set things straight, they'll send Sauveur Emmanuel home in a flash! Because they don't kid around with discipline when they get started.

Especially Augustine. Émilienne's right. Augustine is scary; she's like a skeleton and it seems like her face is always in shadow, even in full daylight. As if she had an extra layer of skin on her face that kept any emotion, any laughter, any smile from showing. Just sternness and shadow. When she speaks, Emmanuel can be as smug as he likes, but he knows he has to toe the line.

I think the child got them worked up because—even if nobody said so—she's the exact replica of her grandmother, and this flock of women, with their one rooster in the yard, is really devoted to their mother.

So when a little spit of a girl can make a whole family jump, can push her mama (who's no pushover) to leave her neighborhood, cross through the darkness of boulevard Hanne, and go down to Assainissement, where she swore she'd never set foot again—when, in addition to that, the child's presence evokes the exact image of your dead mother, it's as if the deceased herself had come in person to tell you, "Enough! There's no time to lose; now you have to straighten out this family and our heritage." The deceased are really attached to this idea of heritage, and when a family tears itself apart, that's the first thing to go.

The sisters must have discussed all that and decided this time to speak to Emmanuel: "What do you think you're doing by not going home to your family for three days? Especially now, when the country is upside down?"

17.

It's time for us to exert control again!

Queen Nono just cuts in without waiting for us to hand things over to her.

Of course the second figure in the quadrille is her favorite: it's just as jumpy and peppery as she is.

Of course the caller says, "Unleash *l'été*! Take your places!" But she ought to know it really isn't about unleashing yourself, but about separating ourselves, one from the other, with grace, to the right beat, and according to the dance's structure.

18.

Just hold on there, you callers! With your permission, I'd like to say how glad I am to hear what this child is teaching us about our country—because I honestly wasn't following along very carefully.

I've been busy trying to find that leg, and with what I was going to tell the Lord on Judgment Day. But, I'm not too worried about that because, besides a few minutes of pride here and there, on the whole I've pretty much walked the straight and narrow.

So this time, it looks like the construction workers have decided to keep protesting, right up to the end. Well, this just makes me think of how long we tolerated being mistreated by our bosses. Instead of a raise, I'd get a present—a shirt, a pair of secondhand shoes—and we were supposed to be grateful. That's what it was like in my time. Maybe I already said that? Thankfully, we had our aid societies. Without them we never would've managed to do a quarter of a quarter of everything we accomplished to better our lives. There weren't any unions; it took a long time for them to come. And the bosses, well, they were the first ones to organize. Those factory bosses had a union all right. They knew you had to be united to get anywhere, but it took us a lot longer to figure that out.

As for me, I never joined a union, even when I worked in a bakery that had one. Maybe I was wrong. Anyhow, those unions, they had some big strikes, and the dead— well, there was a whole pack of them. I heard about those deaths during the union struggles. I don't remember all of them, but in 1910 there were already several: six dead, and a lot wounded at the Saint Marthe factory. I was forty-three, so these aren't childhood memories or stories people told me. There were deaths in 1930 as well, and in '52. Unions won some of the battles, but I always counted on my mutual aid societies and tontines. That's why you have neighborhoods, friendship, and family. You can't joke about that—no, you can't!

19.

That's enough, Nono! We really have to move this story along and listen to the other musicians.

So, please, keep quiet!

The time has come for Julien's brother to speak. Julien is the teacher's husband, whom Émile mentioned.

"Yeah, I saw that Julien in front of the police department in the middle of all those people who were yelling because some poor fool had been arrested."

We don't need your comments, Émile. Thank you very much.

We call forth Henri, Julien's brother. We believe he can help us see how Madame Ladal's departure from school is tied to what's happening in our country.

Let him come forward and play his part in one long movement. We're running out of time!

Which instrument? How about maracas or the *siyak*? Small but essential! You can't do without their percussive effects.

One, two, three—let's go, Henri. Transition from *l'été* to *la poule*!

20.

This Thursday, May 25, 1967, as I unfolded my body, stretched, and massaged my lower back after spending hours bent over working the land—and the land is low, my Lord, is it low!—there they were, not moving, right at the top of the field: Colette and my brother Julien.

Both were standing on the edge of the road, on the blinding white limestone, both motionless under a flamboyant tree whose orange-red flowers carpeted the ground. She, in a pale green dress, delicate, stunning against the coral earth, with her black-as-night hair braided down her back, her eyes waiting for the answer to a question that hadn't yet been asked. He, in pants of some inexpensive cotton, a yellowed shirt and straw hat, the latter item born of a long-standing desire to blend in with the peasants. For once, he wasn't speaking.

I made a mental note to tell him just how out of place his hat looked. That's probably what I would have started off with if she hadn't thrown these words in my face: "Henri, I beg you. Please protect Julien. I'll figure out a way to take care of myself."

Anguish—I could hear it in her voice.

How'd she manage to drag my brother out here anyway?

Then him: "I need you to invite Colette to stay; I have too many things to take care of."

He must have been incredibly worried to drive her all the way out here, forty kilometers from Pointe-à-Pitre. That brother of mine who never stopped complaining about my having moved so far away from town, even though he was proud of how I'd successfully "returned to the land."

Caught up in my own thoughts, everything started rushing together, their words devouring my air: gendarmes, political action, unions, fear. Slowly the words formed into sentences.

"Julien has never been careful. It's wearing me out."

"Colette was evaluated yesterday. They're going to make her pay."

Their confessions stirred the beginnings of an argument I didn't think I'd be able to contain.

"Pay what? Pay for how you've riled them up? Who did what? You dare ask that! I'm going to lose my position!"

"A criminal regulation . . ."

"You're not the first . . ."

I didn't want to fall victim to their hysteria, get caught up in their panic. I took a couple of steps backwards, trying to disguise my retreat. Did they notice?

I thought then about how I never allow myself to just stop and look at the sea. So I left behind the green-apple dress and the straw hat that had invaded my farmer's life: my bananas, my harvests of gigantic yams, twisted and covered in little nobs that reminded me of the corns on Grandma's feet. They had invited themselves onto my land just when the sun's brilliance strikes the leaves of the trees and races to the ocean, descending down the hill in the middle of hundreds of banana trees standing at attention and protecting their offspring, as though they'd ambushed a squad of soldiers in training.

The trunks of banana trees always look solid and proud, right up till the first windstorm that bends them almost completely over, tearing up their leaves, turning them into a defeated army, messy and desolate.

Banana trees aren't meant for hurricanes. They can't even stand up to minor winds—sixty kilometers an hour or so.

I turned towards the sea and the faraway islands, all those Saints insolently bathed in light and softness. But I could feel the two silhouettes behind me, their presence strange in that landscape.

"What's going on?" My question was abrupt and meant to signal I'd heard enough—enough talk—and I didn't understand what they were talking about. "Let's try to make sense out of all this. What do you want from me?"

"That's what we've been trying to tell you for the last five minutes, but as usual you weren't listening."

Colette was looking at me as though the sky had fallen. A kind of *we were counting on you and you let us down.*

"Come on, speak up. Out with it!"

"I was evaluated yesterday."

"And it didn't go well?"

"My class was fine, but the meeting afterwards not so good. I'm sure it was all planned in advance. That guy was looking for anything to make trouble for me."

And he found things. It wasn't hard. Colette said as much.

"He only had to glance at the notebook of one of my girls."

It was a sentence about how Napoleon reinstated slavery.

"Are you a historian, madame? You're rewriting history books now?"

A lesson on the civil rights movement in the United States—with some words by Malcolm X: "Every man should be recognized as a man, without trying to find out if he's white, black, red, or tan."

The examiner, then, aggressive, "How long has this been part of the syllabus?"

"What?"

"You want them to think about the current political situation? Why not introduce the Cuban revolution while you're at it!"

And Colette, to us: "I almost told him I was considering it . . ."

"And you've omitted the morning proverb, expressly selected by the rectorate. You've replaced it with a phrase for them to think about. I can't say this was complete idiocy, but madame, when our children enter their classroom, we want them to have a point of ethical reflection that will stay with them for the entire day. Whereas *your* children are given free rein to deal with moral issues themselves. Do you understand what that means?

"And you're studying the first lines of a poem by Sony Rupaire, 'Joue pour moi,' copied out of an issue of *Esprit*. You called him a Guadeloupean poet, but you forgot to mention, madame, that he's best known as a deserter, that his French nationality was stripped from him and that the review from which you extracted that poem has been censored—all of its copies seized by the court!"

"You get the picture," Colette concluded.

While my sister-in-law was giving me details of her conversation with the examiner, Julien came closer. He summed up the whole thing: "I think that's what it was, Henri; that guy was looking for something specific. As though he needed to verify some information he already had. Don't you see? Because really, Henri, do you know many people who've heard of Sony? Or are aware that *Esprit* was censored in 1962? No, no. That guy had too much information. Someone informed on Colette, as if she were a common criminal!"

Gesturing wildly, absolutely livid, pacing to and fro—Julien was the same agitated man he'd been before he shut up enough to let Colette speak. And he had more to say: nobody was going to stop him from confronting that principal in her wig. Everybody knew she had access to the top; they saw her slip into the rector's office every Thursday morning, probably to report on what she knew. And didn't she look like a mongoose, stimulating fear, ready and eager to kill a snake with a swift bite to its neck with her sharp teeth; and didn't that mongoose creep into the office under the stairs while Colette was being interrogated by that coward—him, too, like a mongoose, and that principal ashamed of her frizzy hair! He'd make her talk; he'd be the one to grab her by the neck; she'd be the serpent and he'd be the mongoose. He'd squeeze the air out of her lungs until her body started to convulse every which way, and with her eyes bulging out of their sockets, she'd beg him to stop. That's what you have to do to traitors, make them vomit their guts out. And didn't he already have an idea about how to get into her house. He knew the right time to find her alone: when the courtyard is finally empty and the concierge is in her own house making dinner. Then the principal takes off her wig to cool off what's left of her brain.

"Those shiny nylon helmets are really hot. That's what exhausts the brain, your scalp stuck with hairpins while sweat rolls down your face."

And then he'll make his move; he'll get into the school through the side gate. It's easy to go behind the school, you just have to avoid the shit, because there're a lot of people who like to do their business behind the school. And you have to watch out for the coconut-tree roots, which can trip you up in a second if you're not paying attention. So he'll slip through the iron bars, stay close to the wall with the toilets (another pissy area to get through), creep up the spiral staircase—the big stone one with the faux marble steps. Yeah, that one, so it won't be noisy. Because if he were to try it in the part of the school that's mostly wood, it would be a lot harder. He'll go right up to her apartment and find her seated in one of those faux teak armchairs. She'll be alone. Her husband, a tax collector, won't have come back yet.

"I'll surprise her! I'll make her confess the awful things she did!"

Speechless, Colette and I listened to this torrent of words accompanied by clenched fists, his hat thrown violently to the ground. We didn't dare interrupt; perhaps we were fascinated by his ability to reenact the exact workings of his imagination.

When he finally shut up, I muttered, "No, no, my brother. That's too much. You don't need to do all that."

Colette took advantage of my own objections to add, "I don't think he realizes he'll only get me into worse trouble. Why can't you see that? I think there's something else going on. The idea about that poem is ridiculous."

I suddenly felt the desire to splash cold water on my face. "I'm overheated," I broke in. "Damn these days in May, they're so dry and brutal." I needed an excuse to get away from them, as soon as possible.

I bent over the pail of water I always kept full, a black plastic pail. I studied the plastic as if I'd never seen it before and spent a long time over that troubled water, already dirty because I'd washed my hands in it. I plunged my hands back into the muddy water, water that was almost as hot as my fiery head. But even the hot water did me good. I scrubbed at my face, almost as if I were trying to take the skin off. It calmed me to rub my eyes, my neck, the back of my head.

When I stood up, Colette had come over to me; we were almost face to face. I could see she was begging, and I understood, even if I dreaded my peaceful life being disrupted by their bickering, that I couldn't desert my brother and disappoint Colette.

She picked up her story again.

And she talked. She'd been summoned to the rector's office Thursday morning—a meeting with one of the administrative heads of the state education machine, in a small office under the stairwell. The door left open, the feeling of being scolded like a child. The rectory was packed; Thursday morning, after all. She'd been called in precisely on the most crowded day, despite it not being a school day, with hundreds of people passing through the corridors: colleagues (even her own colleagues needing to solve some administrative problem), parents, students, too, high school students—primarily high schoolers. An open door in a building that echoes like a cathedral. Anybody could get their fill of the conversation, listen in on what that seemingly proud woman and that official with the too-tight black tie (even trying to look casual in short sleeves) had to say.

Of course Colette knew who he was. A local guy, from her own generation, maybe a little older, by three or four years. She'd even danced with him once or twice, at a ball or a wedding; she didn't remember anymore. They'd met several times before this, but now he was treating her as though she were a perfect stranger, an unknown face. She called him by his first name, but he was formal from the start: "Sit down, Madame Ladal. They asked me to see you. Nothing too serious right now, but there could be trouble down the road."

"Trouble? Why?"

"Seditious activities."

That was hilarious. She burst into laughter, of course upsetting the state's representative. A self-important man assigned the supreme task of keeping the enemies of the Republic and the mother country in their place. But just look at how that mulatto was making fun of him!

"You think this is funny? Well let's see how long you keep laughing!"

"I'm sorry. I didn't mean to laugh. But really"—and she called him again by his first name—"to accuse me of *seditious* activities! What does that even mean?"

"You think I don't know what words mean? Are you trying to test me? To mock me?"

"Don't be so sensitive!"

"Sure, that's right—blacks are hypersensitive."

"I'm just as black as you, monsieur."

"I'm not sure we're the same at all, madame."

Every time she opened her mouth, Colette only made it worse, so she decided to keep quiet. But he took offense at that as well.

"Nothing more to say? What am I supposed to write in my report?"

With that, she snapped, lashing out in rapid-fire Creole: "*Makyé sa ou vlé, an byen fouté pa mal!*"

"I don't give a fuck about your report."

That's when I knew she'd gone too far. You can't take back those words, more devastating than any seditious activity.

The official most likely would have been appeased by a little groveling, a confession that she had maybe made a few critiques of the power structure. From that, he would have understood that she wanted a little piece of it: a position somewhere, a bone to chew on, just like him. Then they would have been in the same race, equals somehow. By doing so she would be admitting he was ahead of her, because he already had the position she coveted. She would have recognized his ability to connect her to the labyrinthine power structure of the middle class. Just enough to expect her to be grateful.

That was the role she should have played, but Colette wasn't capable of it, Julien either. Besides, they both despised people who got caught up in that game. Félix Eboué would have said, "Play the game." But not them; they weren't made for compromises that looked like collaboration. Me neither, but I shied away from administrations and state bureaucracies. I wasn't trying to make my living in anything that depended on them.

※

The sun had started to set while we were talking; a shadow was closing in on us. The flamboyant tree we were standing under had stopped complaining about the heat, no more regular sharp little cracking noises. And the bats were about to start their anarchic flying overhead. A few voices had already called out to me as they passed: "How you doin', Henri!"

"Hey, Plumain."

Men were leading their cows back. "Hey, Henri."

"Hey, Girard!"

Knee-high boots, clothes stained with banana sap, huge hats, rubber gloves, and sharp knives had all finished their day's work and were moving slowly away from us. Walking with ease, taking big determined steps.

I asked, "What do we do now?"

"I want Colette to stay with you tonight and all week-end, if need be."

She wouldn't go along with this; *he* was the one who needed protection. I didn't exactly feel like spending my evening listening to increasingly crazy stories. I knew all the bad aspects of my brother: his penchant for useless provocation, his ability to piss off every kind of imaginable authority, his stubbornness and fury—angering even the people in the various political groups he frequented, without missing a meeting. I would have happily welcomed Colette into my home, but she was having none of it. There was no way she'd leave him by himself when she could help keep him from encountering an armed policeman in some dark alley.

My brother mumbled, "All this way for nothing."

"That's not true," she answered, smiling.

I invited them up to the house for a drink, but she avoided answering. She whispered to me later, when I leaned into the car to say goodbye, "If we'd gone into your house, he'd convince you to keep me there, and I don't want him to leave for La Pointe alone. I'm really worried, you know."

When they left for La Pointe, I started to gauge how dangerous it was, especially for him. I'd heard from friends that that Friday was going to be messy, and I figured he'd for sure be one of the first persons the authorities would go after.

Our mother was especially worried about him, and I was too. One of Colette and Julien's neighbors, whose balcony looked onto their inner courtyard, told me about his tirades against the government. His provocations as well.

Those inner courtyards are the best thing about Pointe-à-Pitre. They're a little like a port: you land there after a long day, half-dead from life in the noisy and dirty city, sit down in the cool shade underneath a tree, and then you have a little rum or some ice-cold lemon soda with anisette liqueur—or both, the fiery rum followed by the pleasure of an icy drink—and watch the sun hurry on down. People who don't have a courtyard sit on their stoops or on a bench they've brought out front, or on a rocking chair installed like a sentinel in front of their door. Some have folding chairs they take out only to fold them up again and store them behind the door. Others end the day in the backrooms of shops, inhaling the smells of dried cod or gasoline.

Everybody finds a way to enjoy this blessed lapse of time separating the blindingly bright days from the deep lightless nights, nights overtaken by the hordes of stray dogs that sweep through town. Everybody enjoys dusk in their own way, but nothing's as good as a courtyard aperitif.

The neighbor who's observing Julien at my request has often enjoyed that little moment of early evening calm at their place, under the breadfruit tree.

He told me it's not easy to get Julien to shut up; he's so chatty, so ready to tell the world what he thinks about France meddling in our country's politics. Nothing can stop him. Trying to keep him from going too far, Colette does her part by gushing about her favorite class, her thirty-two little schoolgirls.

My spy said that Colette knows her students so intimately that when she begins to describe them, it feels like you're looking at a photo that's just been taken.

Everybody who's enjoyed the shade of the breadfruit tree in my brother's courtyard knows all about how little Maryvonne struggles to avoid making holes in the pages of her notebook, how she tries to stop spotting her face with purple ink. Everybody finds it funny and at the same time a little pathetic, everybody except Julien, who's troubled by ridiculing the disadvantaged.

Julien is the kind of man devoted to the rights of the most humble—"the poorest of the poor," "workers ferociously exploited by colonialism"—and he wouldn't stand for anyone making fun of their failures or limitations. He certainly wasn't going to allow his wife to be one of "the vectors of cultural alienation."

But she'd just smile, shrug her shoulders as though she were annoyed. She thought he maybe went too far, but she would never not stand by him in the fights he and his comrades engaged in.

Was Julien a socialist, a communist, a nationalist, for autonomy, for independence? Even I didn't know how to classify him anymore. Regardless, he was somebody that no administration or bureaucracy could stomach.

My brother wasn't afraid of anything. Or you could say, and I will, he just didn't have any sense of the word "caution." Everybody warned him to cool it, but it was hopeless. He insisted his political loyalties be known and accepted by everyone.

If I had to describe him, what would I say?

Julien was a voice. Yeah, that's what he was, a voice

that careened towards you from the end of the street even before he started walking down Commandant Mortenol to La Place de la Victoire, where he lived. A voice that interrogated children who fell into his clutches: "What the hell are you doing in the street? Just where are the parents of these children?"

A voice that was amplified by a thunderous laugh whenever he encountered Panpan, an enormous dock-worker who sweated rum and introduced himself by imitating the sound of a fire truck, echoing the words of a popular song: "*M'wen ni on loto nèf, pin-pon, pin-pon, pin-pon, pam-pam.*" Some people, liking all the musical sounds, also called him Pinpon.

I met Panpan in their courtyard. A colossal figure— you'd better get out of his way—because one of his feet, looking bleached and dried from what leaked out of the cement sacks he carried all day long across the docks, was as big and heavy as a cinder block. Nobody wants to have that land on his own *zaïgos*, not even when you wear shoes.

Julien and Panpan were equals when it came to their vocal prowess. Yes, indeed they were! Except Panpan's voice was a lot rougher than Julien's. But they were thick as thieves, even if Panpan said only nasty things about the communists and all their buddies. It seemed he had a free hand in the house, and the fact he could say what-ever he liked about the Party could be explained by Julien's absolute conviction: "The working class is alienat-ed. It's up to us to help it get ahead."

If Panpan was any kind of example, the working class had serious troubles with alcohol. But did that poor fellow even know he was part of the class in question, or even that he was alienated?

One time I was sitting with Panpan under the breadfruit tree. There he was, sweating like a pig in his torn undershirt, his enormous khaki shorts hanging off his body, when, with eyes riveted on the tree and hands on his stomach, I heard him say, "Gotta cut this *fouyapenla*; it's gonna tilt up your house and one day you'll be sleepin' with the roots, Madame Colette. They'll be in your bed!"

I always wondered how Colette could be so easygoing about letting him into their home. No fuss, Colette—always leaving behind the delicious scent of eau de cologne, Reine des Fleurs. I liked to imagine my sister-in-law making Panpan sit in a big silver tub of water, scrubbing him briskly with a grass brush and spraying him with Héliotrope Blanc, the men's version of her royal perfume. In the daydream I had, I saw Panpan groaning with pleasure while Julien railed against the old Easter tradition of bringing street people home, washing them, cleaning them up, putting fresh clothes on their backs, and then releasing them again to the streets, to their delirium and their wanderings, until the next festival of Christian charity.

Because Colette was a good Christian, she taught the neighborhood children catechism on Thursday afternoons, and I know the priest was proud of her, even if he scolded her for marrying that crazed Castro supporter. Colette and the priest argued incessantly about Julien. My mother told me all about it.

Colette would protest, "A Castro supporter? Do you

see a beard anywhere? I don't even like men with beards; they itch, and I don't like to see them scratch their necks and their chins."

"Well maybe he doesn't have his beard, but he certainly has his ideas. Yes, he does."

Eventually Colette thought up the best argument for getting the priest to stop lecturing her once and for all: "You're the first priest I ever heard of who wanted to tear asunder what the Good Lord joined together."

Bingo! Father Anselme stopped his attempts at persuading her that Julien was nothing more than a mad good-for-nothing she should never have married. No more discussions, just some teasing once in a while. "How's your communist? Does he have a beard yet? How's it coming in?"

Though, if Colette had let him, Julien would have dressed himself up as the perfect Castro revolutionary, donning beard, cap, olive drab military uniform, or that Cuban shirt we call *alcora*, but they call *guayabera*. But she kept an eye on him, and he pretty much kept himself in check with that kind of thing. From time to time, he'd disguise himself as a peasant when he went off to feed the few animals he kept, wearing that same bizarre straw hat from yesterday—just before my stupid accident along l'Allée Dumanoir.

As for the rest, Colette didn't get involved in the speeches, the meetings, the conventions at the Mutualité, the communist pamphlets distributed at the end of mass, the closed-door political workshops—even though he couldn't stop himself from telling her certain things.

My brother spoke so loudly that his words could be

heard by the gendarmes drinking their aperitif on the doctor's balcony next door—those police officers with a vested interest in the suspicious happenings of the Ladal courtyard. But while Julien raised his voice and yelled, Colette would whisper, calming him down. Whereas Julien encouraged his guests to stay to listen to his ideas, Colette would try to send them home, gently suggesting, "My friends, it's time for dinner."

How many different strategies did she invent when those imposing calves in their white socks appeared on the doctor's balcony? Those big white legs of the law were an omen, a guarantee that a terrible and unavoidable tragedy was about to befall them. So she'd pick up the glasses and invite everyone inside, justifying herself by saying, "Don't you think it's getting a little cold out here?"

She'd pull the salon door shut behind her and close the shutters, and everyone would settle into wooden armchairs with fake red-leather cushions. A collection of shiny blue-marbled animals was scattered around the room, looking straight ahead, their eyes empty. Sometimes she even sent Julien over to our mother's. "Weren't you supposed to go see your mother today?"

Or she'd ask about the animals he was pasturing in a rental property in Besson, just outside Pointe-à-Pitre. How about the chickens, the cow, the goats? Didn't he have to feed and water them? What about the grass for the rabbits in their hutch?

"Don't you want to go with him, Panpan?"

Panpan would have done anything to keep sitting comfortably squeezed in that armchair that was too low for his legs, in that salon that was too small for his size. Nevertheless, he went with Julien, who was never fooled by Colette's maneuvering and who'd always yell out one last explosive thought, "One of these days those people will have to find their way back to their own country and leave ours to us!"

The gendarmes' hands would linger distractedly near their hips, barely touching the pistols hanging there in their worn brown holsters.

Julien let them have it, "And when they've killed enough of us, as though we were rabbits, they'll even get a medal."

Colette would push him out the door as quickly as she could. "Monsieur Panpan is waiting for you, Julien . . ."

"Yeah, fine, let's go."

And Panpan would drag Julien away from the chance of getting hit by a stray bullet.

Sometimes when it was even too late for dinner, when the gendarmes' calves had already made their appearance, when all other strategies failed, Colette made one last attempt to make all the guests leave. She'd gather up the notebooks she had to correct and pronounce, "I have to look over the homework I've given to my students."

✳

Thanks to my friend, I knew everything threatening my brother and my sister-in-law. But if they'd come all the way out to see me, it meant that even my reckless brother had realized something bad was going to happen.

I had to intervene and ask someone to protect them. I still had a few friends from high school who held important positions, especially in the police. Our country is so small we sometimes find help from the most unlikely places; unsuspected friends can countermand the most draconian laws.

I jumped into my car, but I never arrived in La Pointe. A gory accident put an end to my journey towards town. I lost my head in that terrible collision; it was severed at the neck and landed in the middle of the banana plantation near l'Allée Dumanoir.

I hate that road, have always despised it, especially because of all the trees bordering the narrow, buckling asphalt—four hundred nasty royal palms. Twelve hundred meters of one-hundred-year-old trees, which shelter the nearby banana plants from the ocean winds, winds that were blowing fantastically when I crashed my car into a royal palm.

Let me describe how the leaves shook, how the branches scraped the car, how, unable to withstand the shock, the palm tree tumbled to the ground and seemed to bounce a few meters away, sounding just like an eraser hitting the floor.

My life stopped on that road. If I'd lived one more day, maybe I would have died on La Place de la Victoire. The inevitable was just waiting to catch up with me, so it seems.

But death, old and stubborn, showed up a day early. And so, in the end, I never found out what happened to Colette and Julien. I even wonder if my presence tonight in Émilienne's courtyard has any meaning at all.

THE THIRD FIGURE: *LA POULE*

1.

Begging your pardon, dear readers, dear dancers, dear dancing readers. Today we'll be what you might call *entrepreneurial* callers.

This Friday merits some wiggle room in our usual manner of calling.

There's been so much commotion, it's impossible for the music not to be affected.

Friday, May 26, our little sister Émilienne came home a good half hour late.

It was noontime.

We thought she'd been lingering near La Place de la Victoire. She really loves that spot with its hundred-year-old sandbox trees, which they say were planted to commemorate the abolition of slavery.

Whenever she leaves school, where the pungent stench of piss from the Turkish toilets overpowers the sea air, she often stops for a few minutes on La Place. She closes her eyes, and while the other children around her run, laugh, and fight with one another, she greedily inhales the heady aroma of midday tide.

Oh yes, how she loves the smell of the sea!

So we thought it was only her usual seaside pause that had kept her away.

Mama was getting ready to scold her, as she did every afternoon.

But when she arrived, we were immediately alarmed by

her torn dress and broken glasses, the traces of tears on her cheeks. To tell the truth, we were shattered.

Our mother grabbed her, holding her close to the dampness of a housedress smelling of dishwater.

She was sobbing like she does when we're mean and pinch her.

But for once we weren't guilty of anything, and we couldn't understand the reason behind her enormous sorrow.

We watched her hiccup, "Our teacher has disappeared." And even though we'd always preferred to laugh at her melodramatic suffering, this time we might have had tears in our eyes. I say "might" because nobody really ly knows if our memories of this particular afternoon haven't already been altered by our new circumstances. We're waiting.

Our mother gave Émilienne permission to take refuge in our parents' big bed. In the middle of the day! Getting high on the scent of ylang-ylang that our father always left in his wake.

She had wanted to sleep like the dead, to forget everything. But in the end, she couldn't even close her eyes.

Smiling at us, she let us tease her about her midday siesta. She liked Mama's joke, suggesting she have her morning coffee as if she'd just woken up. As if it were early in the morning, time for bread dunked in weak, sugary coffee.

We saw her smile, and that small hint of her normal tender self made us think we'd saved her from disaster.

All of us—yes, all of us—were ready to give her permission to go back to school, even after having gone to bed at that strange hour.

She would leave with the hope her teacher would be there after lunch break.

Mama thought she'd slept some, but we watched her like a hawk, as we always did, and we knew she didn't close her eyes even once.

She's our favorite, our littlest, who we're unkind to sometimes, of course, but who we also fuss over constantly.

No, she didn't fall asleep.

She was almost drunk from having cried so much, so she listened to the radio dispense vague information on the construction workers' strike and on the negotiations that were "coming along."

The announcer spoke in a monotone, the emphasis of his words falling repetitively, like a lullaby.

Indifferent to his litany, we instead paid attention to our mother, who was beating or stirring something—probably a puree—incorporating butter into potatoes or into boiled breadfruit, her wooden spoon hitting the same spot at the same pace.

Our little sister turned to look out the window, watching the sun filter through the shutters, the slats of light projected on the walls; she concentrated on the wavering shadows, on the warmth in which she normally takes comfort.

She always says that heat's as comforting as a hot bowl of milk. That makes us laugh, but it's true all the same! She's still pretty naive, our Émilienne, and very fragile. We should have protected her.

But we allowed her to fight the violence in this country all by herself—the brutality of it all battering her about, scattering her like ashes in the wind. She alone had to reckon with the disappearance of the teacher she and her classmates loved so much. Her rage had reduced her to silence, without her understanding the bigger danger her teacher posed to the men in navy blue or gray-striped suits, those joyless white men who looked to us like an enemy tribe.

She didn't know it, but every one of us had at one point or another encountered those men in suits, sitting silently in the back of our classrooms, obsessed with discovering the tipping point in the battle to learn that teachers wage with their students.

We should have told her that examiners don't get rid of teachers permanently but transfer them somewhere else, to another school that she could maybe visit one day.

We never thought she'd prefer facing death over finding herself face-to-face with the empty void where there'd once been a teacher's desk, confronted with an empty cupboard, the dissolution of all her routines, as if by magic—a death, then, more unreal than all those that happened around her that afternoon.

We let her go back to school, hoping as she did that it was all just a simple mistake to be easily resolved. But that was an illusion, because everything was far more terrible than we could have imagined.

Luckily, Guy-Albert, one of Papa's workers, was there. He'll be the only one to dance in this last figure of the quadrille, *la poule*. Just him, all by himself. Guy-Albert has the floor for his story and his drum. And our little one will keep on shaking her tambourine.

To the floor, good fellow!

2.

A simple honest man, that's how people have always thought of me. A simple honest man. A poor man among poor men, that too. An odd way to see someone. How do you ever escape that sort of ironclad box, once you've been put in it? Even when you start suffocating, even when you feel more and more trapped. It's not always enough to use your imagination. You long to be different from what you've always seemed to be.

I've just about had it with being that simple and honest man, the poor man among poor men, who waits every morning on the side of the road to be picked up by his boss in a truck. The easygoing and uncomplicated man climbs into the back and finds a place among the other workers whose speech is broken because they're seated over a worn-out suspension and the road's rocky. Nothing distracts that simple man from the drive to the work site with its dust, the noise of machines carelessly tearing up the land, the merciless sun.

Every morning, leaving the house at dawn, taking off on foot, crossing through the part of town that's still asleep, tackling the coast until he gets to the main road, and then waiting for the boss, standing on one leg like a great *kyo*, a heron resting from a long trip. Or leaning against a tree, shouldering a cloth sack with water in a metal thermos, a lunch pail, an old towel—those three indispensable items that simple and honest boys know to bring, having resigned themselves to following their father's strict advice (learn to handle a trowel, that's sure to be useful) and to their mother's prediction (my poor boy, you'll never amount to a thing, one day you'll end up in construction with a leaky thermos, a beat-up lunch box, and a frayed towel to wipe away your sweat).

Every morning, my boss Absalon lays on his horn as if he's crazed, and I always think, without even glancing at the faded blue truck, that his stinginess runs on gas fumes alone, yes. I wonder why he needs to make such a scene so early in the morning, when he knows I'm right there waiting, when he can see me standing there from far away.

He brakes way too hard, and I wonder if the sharp screech coming from the truck is from relief or exhaustion. It gets on my nerves.

"*Ka sa yé, Guy-Albè?*"

"*Ka sa yé, patron?*"

"How ya doin'?" That's how it goes. We don't talk much, nothing personal in any case.

3.

On Thursday night, I sleep with Mama.

She's the one who invited me. I'm still a little anxious because of what I said to her today, because of the visit to Papa's sisters, but after dinner, she calls me over.

She's still seated at her place at the table.

She kisses me on my eyelids. She likes to give us wet kisses on our eyes, and I like it too, a lot, even if it tickles.

"Let's stop being mad at each other, okay? You can sleep with me tonight."

I'm so comfortable. I sleep with her soft warm breasts against my back.

When I wake up on Friday, I'm calm, even if I can see you didn't come home again last night.

☀

Friday, May 26, 1967. I'm going to school, and I'm sure my teacher will be there. I'm going to write the date in my notebook. I pack my book bag. I remember to grab my report card from behind the green filing cabinet.

Marlyse waits for me on the corner of rue Vatable; we always walk together. I don't tell her about the visit to my aunts. I didn't tell anybody about it, not even Emmy. I want to keep it inside me, deep down inside, because it makes me happy.

I say to Marlyse, "All joy has not withered away!" And she looks at me with big eyes. She thinks I've gone nuts.

I laugh and start to run, saying over and over again, "All joy is not lost, all joy is not lost . . ."

We cross La Place de la Victoire, and the shutters of Madame Ladal's house are open. Another good sign. I repeat my new song, jumping up and down with my book bag.

At La Place, there are men speaking in front of the subprefecture, and lots of kids, like usual: students from my school, girls from the Michelet High School, boys from Carnot, and some students from the Catholic school, wearing their white blouses and their red-and-black checked skirts. (They always cross La Place without speaking to us. To them, we're just savages, a bunch of *bamous*.)

4.

Once I thought the boss and I could become close, so I decided he should be godfather to my last kid, I mean the one I had two years ago. A little girl. He came to the baptism with his whole family and some money for a present: a small envelope, not exactly stuffed with bills, more like something thin and cutting, like a razor. After that, nothing. Except, when he manages to think about it, he might ask, "*Tout moun-la byen?*"

I always say fine, everybody in the family's just fine.

And then we talk about turf, stones, gravel, asphalt, and drywall. Always rushed. Pick up the workers on the side of the road, drop them off at the work site, give a couple of orders, make sure all the material's been delivered, and then, take off!

Not that we need him there. It's normal for him to leave the work site. Sometimes he's got a bunch of jobs going on at once, in communes that aren't close together at all. We still don't understand why he drives everyone on his construction teams himself, but we suspect he'd rather run himself into the ground with that stupid task than pay us a transportation stipend, which some other bosses allow. Sometimes he lets his handyman, Michel, drive, and he at least doesn't plow through our sector like a tank on a country road. He knows how to wait, quietly, if by chance a work buddy is running a little late.

We prefer it when the boss is off our backs and not complaining about how the communes don't pay him. He's always mouthing off about taxes, the Bureau of Equipment, and all those public offices hounding him and—we always know what's coming next—"stealing the bread from his workers' mouths."

If you don't get what that means for your pay period—that you're *not* getting any—you're either thick, naive, or an asshole.

When he starts to talk like that, we workers just mutter things like "uh-huh" or we suck our teeth, but nobody dares say anything.

But he always ends up giving us what we're owed. He'll set up his little table and folding chair, install himself under a shade tree, and pull a fat envelope stuffed with bills out of his shabby briefcase.

On those days, he thinks we don't notice how he sets up all kinds of blinds to protect himself, as though, for as long as we've been working for him, we'd ever try to steal his money—it's ours, after all. As soon as the piles are lined up, the bills secured with a rubber band, our pay doesn't belong to him anymore; but he doesn't see it that way. As far as he's concerned, it will always be his money, even when it ends up in our pockets.

The last time it happened, the best thing he could cook up was to put a pistol in the glove box of his Dauphine and ask one of us, Albéri, I remember, to go fetch his glasses from the car.

Of course Albéri came back screaming, "Hey Boss, that's not some little cap gun you got in your glove box!"

And the boss, crafty as a fox, "Well you never know, what if I run across a mongoose?"

What the hell kind of mongoose would that be? I wondered. A two-fisted and two-footed mongoose who does construction work on your sites! Who do you think you are, Absalon? You better watch out that pistol doesn't get used against you, against Absalon, the big mongoose. That's not the first time I gave him a nickname, but I thought "mongoose" really fit him, even if it's a pretty common insult around here. The way the mongoose darts along so fast, the way it crosses the road like a bat out of hell as if the devil himself were after it, the way it doesn't trust anything around it. Well, that's the spitting image of our boss, Sauveur Emmanuel Absalon.

What's his problem? Why doesn't he trust us? I know the guy, and I don't even know how close he is to the other workers who've been with him for at least ten years, who saw the birth of his last little girl, who went to his mother's funeral, who bring him fruit from their gardens, who invite him home to eat, who give him the seat of honor at their local festivals—and he pulls that pistol stunt on us! I guess it's because he's such a coward because when Almighty God was doling out courage, you sure can't say Absalon was first in line!

So what does he do instead? Yell, of course. The kind of yelling cowards always keep close to their chest, ready to be launched defensively, before even starting a discussion, before speaking like men who respect each other and aren't afraid. Instead, he barks; he barks a lot, a whole *krèy*!

And since the end of last year, he's yelled all the time because we asked for a little raise.

Christmas and New Year's Day were already in full

swing, not just in stores, but in our kids' heads and in our wives' needling: it's time to change the linoleum in the big room and the bedroom, time to put some new curtains over the doorways—that's the style here, curtains made of colored plastic strips that wave in the wind and make a kind of noise that lulls you to sleep—time to buy new shoes for one of the kids. You know, what you always do at New Year's, those little things that bring good luck for the coming year. Everything had already been discussed with our families, and our wives kept hounding us that we just had to ask for a small raise with our next pay.

But where the hell were we going to find the courage to convince a man like that? Bowing and scraping in front of a guy who knows exactly how to respond: He has a family too. He, too, has children. He knows, just like us, when the holidays arrive and the little ones always want new things, how difficult it is to say no when they touch your face and make you look right into their eyes and promise.

"Especially my little girl. She does it so good. Her mother tells me I don't know how to say no, but isn't it always my wife who says to the child, 'Ask your daddy.' Isn't she the one after all?"

"Boss, here's how it is. It's the end of the year, you know the holidays are coming; we'd really like to give just a little more to the family, it's hardly anything at all."

But he knows everything about us, "And what about that pig you're going to butcher and sell?"

"But Boss, that's our personal business. We've been

working for you for a lot of years now, and it's been a real long time since we had a raise."

In the beginning, it's like a game. We know each other. We smile. We even promise him a kilo of meat for his family: real good meat, fed with green bananas, delicious, mouth-watering, *koupé dwèt*!

We laugh a little and then he says, "I'll see what I can do, but you know how it is: taxes, city halls that don't pay me when they should, the cost of building materials, the suppliers who're always after me. You can't reason with them, you know . . ."

Quite the performance.

After a week goes by, we bring it up again and he blows up. And since then, he's been yelling nonstop, *a kontinyé*, like he's trying to keep us from speaking, like he wants to intimidate us so much we won't dare mention our next pay and the raise.

Christmas went by, *joud'lan* too.

He only paid us part of what he owed; we'll have to wait for the rest. Same old song.

"I don't have the money. I'm waiting for the prefecture to give me the rest. It's on its way. A friend is helping me out. You have to have people in place when you work with the government. You always have to know somebody. They pay the big guys first. Everything they owe them. Cash on the barrelhead. The big construction companies carry weight, but us little guys, we have to fight. We practically have to be drowning before we get any action. And then there's that old crone who's holding up the dockets because her daughter . . . Anyhow, it's a long story, but men, you know how nasty our fellow citizens can be, especially women. That's why, if it were up to me, I'd be an American. You know I really am like an American, just not like a black one; I'm helping you guys carry the weight of your skin!"

But the money never came, so one day in January, after the holidays, I went to their house and took their radio, that big radio they had in their living room. I went in and said I'd return it when he gave me the money he owed me. He wasn't home, and his wife watched me do what I had to do without saying a word.

We know each other pretty well, her and me, because sometimes I work on their house. Every time the boss has a little extra cash, he does some more construction. He already has two floors, but the second one needs to be finished, and he's thinking about a third.

Madame Emmanuel doesn't talk much, but she's good to us. She brings us a glass of cool water when we've been swallowing too much dust, sand, and cement.

She knew I respected her, even if I was taking their radio.

So when I was almost out the door, she says to me, "I understand, Guy-Albert. But try to understand too. It's difficult for him, and hard for us as well. Not all the time, as it is for you, I know that, but if he's telling you he doesn't have the money, it's true. If you want the radio, take it. I understand."

My wife and I spent some quality time enjoying that brown and tan radio. In the evenings, we picked up all kinds of information in our bedroom, with the radio sitting next to our bed.

We covered it with a table runner during the day to keep the dust out, protecting it just like I'd found it, under a cloth, the day I carried it out of Emmanuel Absalon's house.

Every night we uncovered it and turned the dials very carefully, traveling to unknown cities and listening to foreign languages and music we'd never heard before. For a whole week, my wife and I tasted the magic of voices in the night, glued to each other—well, my wife was pressed against my back to better hear the words coming from the other side of the bed, from on top of my nightstand.

It's from listening to all those voices and all that news from everywhere imaginable that I started to understand why I didn't really feel complete—as if there were too many things I didn't know.

And it was when I was turning the two big dials next to the speaker—watching the needles pass over the list of all those little names painted in white on the channel finder—that I realized we were trapped on a little piece of land, with the sea chewing at every side, shrinking because of the waves; nearly underwater with no way of getting out. Even the radio's crackling seemed to be coming from underwater.

But at the same time, my wife and I had some real good laughs! Boy did we laugh when we discovered they were talking about us in cities real far away, in regions of France we'd never heard of, like that time we heard a farmer from Béarn. Where the hell is Béarn? He grew yams. You had to hear that radio guy ask what they looked like!

"It's like a morning glory," and my wife says, "What's a morning glory?"

"And the leaves are like ivy." My wife says, "What do ivy leaves look like?"

"Well, I guess they look like yam leaves," I say.

"It's almost like a grapevine." (Grapevine?) *"You attach them to iron spikes with wire. It tastes sort of like a potato, a new potato, the most expensive ones."* (Oh come on!) *"It cooks up easy and is quite delicate."*

"So what does it look like? What if I told you it looks like the cudgel Hercules carried over his shoulder?" (Really, a cudgel with little hairs sprouting out of its end? I mean, really, little hairs?)

Well I supposed this amused their listeners. Anyhow, it sure made us laugh!

"There's not much of a market for yams in France. But students from Martinique"—(hey, what about Guadeloupe?)—*"from North Africa and from sub-Saharan Africa are always happy to see products they're used to eating at home. And I think they'd be very good for people who have restricted diets. Because yams don't absorb much fat, they're really easy to digest."* Wow, the things we learned. *"And you can accompany yams with a white wine from the region."*

My wife and I listened hungrily to that radio, right up till the day the gendarmes came for it.

It wasn't Madame Emmanuel who called them. She would never have done that.

When they knocked on the door, they were pretty polite. After all I'd always been an easy law-abiding guy. It was the first time my boss had issued an official complaint against me, and they knew me a little from the neighborhood . . . We'd even crossed paths at the corner store on Mayoute. They knew I wasn't somebody who'd make a scene, and as long as I gave the radio back without making any trouble, they'd hold nothing against me. I didn't resist, but I was sorry to see that radio go. We didn't even have time to use the record player attached to the top. It was under a little cover that raised up when you hooked it to a folding metal rod.

So I gave back the radio, but I realized we'd crossed a line, Absalon and me.

That's why I threatened him, *"An ké fann kyou aw on jou! Révolvè-la ou ni an vwati aw-la, défyé'w pou i pa sèvi pou'w menm!"*

Obviously he fired me. I would have fired myself! What kind of person threatens to kill somebody like that? He didn't hire me back for two whole weeks, and I couldn't find any other work. But Madame Emmanuel and my wife sorted it out. The wives managed to calm us down.

"Guy-Albert, we need that work and Boss Absalon isn't as bad as all that."

So we talked it out, just the two of us, in private, man

to man. He hired me for another job. But when he yells now, I don't pay him any mind because he knows I'm no *tèbè*, not the dumbass he thought I was. I saw in his eyes he's afraid of me! Sometimes he'll still yell at me in front of the other guys, just to show them who's boss.

But I know how scared he is so I'm leaving a door open for him. That's the way it is: you always have to prepare an exit for your enemy, so he won't turn into a wild beast. The door's cracked open, and as long as he lowers his eyes, he can yell as much as he wants.

5.

The principal is waiting for us at the entrance to the school.

She grabs us by the arms, all of Madame Ladal's thirty-two students; she digs her super-long nails into our flesh and corners us against the wall in her office.

I start thinking about what we'd yelled at the concierge on Wednesday. We took off like lightning, and neither the principal nor Madame Parize tried to catch us. But now we're going to get it!

I don't try to fight the principal, but some of my classmates do.

Elizabeth pulls her arm away and screams, "What's going on?"

The principal doesn't answer, so the students huddle closer together. We pout like clown fish while the other classes line up outside to go into their classrooms.

The concierge is hanging on to the long rope attached to the big bell in the courtyard. She's ringing and ringing it, and while I watch her, I remember everything our teacher taught us about the school bell: "Words have a lot of different meanings. For example, a bell has a brain, a lower lip, shoulders, a belly, and a robe."

I also remember how she forgot to draw the bell on the board so we could put labels on where the brain, the lip, the shoulders, the belly, and the robe were all located.

Our teacher isn't anywhere in the courtyard. We look at each other; we say to ourselves: she isn't here. I try with all my might to accept it, but I can't.

When all the teachers have gone up to their rooms, the principal calls out our names from her big book of students and she separates us into little groups.

"The first ten students will go to Madame Desravins's class."

Nobody moves.

"Do you hear me? From Absalon to Chathuant."

But nobody moves.

6.

It's always on a Saturday morning that we do it—kill the pig, I mean. Early morning, just when the sun rises. Sometimes everybody in the neighborhood's still asleep, but we always tell them the night before. Tomorrow is the pig's day. That way the animal's squeals don't catch them unawares.

This year I decided that Julien Ladal, a red-haired guy who rents some land next to my pigpens, should be part of the gang—my neighbors and my family—who gets a share of the pig. That is, I could sell him some, because we don't really give it away; we sell. I haven't known the man for long, but he's already become someone I trust; my people, so to speak.

It happened as though it was always meant to. I'd seen him arrive and get his animals settled. He knew what he was doing with them, even if he was a city man from La Pointe. And that was easy to see when he spoke: too loud. That was the first thing. He spoke too loud like he had to drown out some kind of noise inside himself; and whatever the mess was, it had to be goddamn powerful, because you could hear him talk from the top of the hill when he was tying his cow up at the bottom—even if it was just the cow he was talking to, saying God knows what. Except sometimes he came with another really big fellow who spoke even louder than he did.

And he had this hat, a brand-new straw hat that was too big. One of those *bacoua* hats that make guys think they look like a real peasant, except that we don't wear *bacouas*. That's what guys in Martinique wear, so you notice it. Where the hell did he pick that up from?

Anyhow, we weren't going to get mad at him because he had the wrong hat; maybe somebody gave it to him. You can't judge a guy by his hat, but we couldn't stop ourselves from making fun of him a little.

Our friendship formed slowly.

I hadn't realized it until I met him, but I was lonely. I mean, I really felt all alone in the world. I didn't know what was wrong, but my buddies said I was "morose," that was the word they used: *"Guy-Albè, ou ka sanm sa ki moròz!"*

Morose? I guess I was. It wasn't that I didn't like my life, only that everything seemed a little empty to me.

When I came home from work in the early afternoons, I was clean. I'd showered. Even if I had some limestone dust on my black skin, you could see I was clean. I had the right to sit down in front of the plate my wife had put on the table, covering it with another plate or a white cloth. I'd earned the right to have my meal, to sit down under my own roof and stretch out for a little nap before leaving at the end of the afternoon to take care of the pigs, and maybe have a drink with my buddies at the corner store.

I had all that in my life: a roof, a wife, children, work, but I still felt empty.

When that emptiness reared its head in plain daylight, when it was so clear my heart plunged into my stomach and I got weak in the knees, well, then I didn't even feel like talking. Couldn't even enjoy the joking, the laughs that help you get through the sadness when nature is too calm, when the morning is dead silent, when the hills are still covered up by fog.

Enough of the jokes, enough bursts of anger after a couple of glasses too many, enough *wouklaj*—because complaining doesn't get you anywhere.

When Julien showed up in his *bacoua* hat, I shied away from him at first, but then I saw he was a good guy, really: not a bit mean, always ready to lend a helping hand, drive a woman to town, bring back something for a neighbor, accept your offer of a drink without making a big deal of it and without drinking the whole bottle like he was dying of thirst, and not minding at all if you took some of his grass for your own rabbits: "I don't have any trouble with it as long as you don't mind watering my animals when I'm not here."

In other words, a good neighbor. So when I decided to slaughter that pig, I suggested he enjoy it too—real good meat, cheaper than at the butcher's shop, and always weighed so you get a little bit more for your money.

And he, too, started slowly telling me about his life, especially about the union. I usually didn't trust union guys, didn't even know why. I liked my own space, as they say, I liked being by myself. Even my work buddies . . . I didn't spend that much time with them, just the bare minimum so they wouldn't take me for a snob, calling me an "aristocrat," the way they do here.

"Unions are good, you know, so you don't have to stand up to your boss all by yourself."

When he said that, I kept thinking of Absalon and all the little issues I needed to bring up with him. At the same time, he didn't really feel like the kind of boss Julien, my new friend, was talking about: a boss who gets rich, who mistreats his workers, who makes a huge profit—a *capitalist*.

I'd known Absalon for such a long time, it seemed that even if he wanted to build himself a big house, in the end, he was more like me, with nine kids to provide for. I didn't see how Julien could cut everybody from the same cloth.

I told him that: "You shouldn't put all the hens in the same chicken coop."

I had a point. That's what he said. He listened to me speak and thought about my ideas; he wasn't one of those guys who has all the questions and all the answers, and all the ballots to shove into the ballot box.

He could change his mind if what he was thinking didn't correspond to what you'd experienced in real life.

We often sat down to gab, just the two of us, under a tree. I didn't want him to come to my house too often, didn't want people in the neighborhood to say I was turning into a communist. Because, and that's how it goes—and how it went—it only took two or three comments in the back room of the corner shop on Mayoute for everybody who was a Besson communist to start saying that Julien was a strange one, not really fish not really foul, kind of in the Party and kind of not. More like a dissident.

"A fella who talks too much."

That's what Célaure concluded. He was one of the

faithful and knew Julien a little, but as they say, their dogs weren't in the same race.

I wasn't going to start an argument with Célaure, so I got out of there.

As far as I was concerned, they could take their political parties and shove them. I didn't want anything to do with them. Nothing. I wasn't afraid of having ideas, that wasn't it, but what I wanted . . . well, I knew it had nothing to do with a party, with a vote, with a poster you put up, with a tract you hand out.

What I wanted was to make some progress, so I kind of liked this idea of a union. It meant I could join others to get the things we all knew we should have. Back then, I never thought I'd end up facing a bunch of gendarmes, like when I took the boss's radio.

In fact, it was Potiron who took me to my first meeting. Léon Potiron, the head of the new work site the boss had assigned me to. A guy who didn't talk much, like me. A guy who didn't always have a new joke to tell. Hey, fellas, you heard this one? A guy goes into a bakery to buy a loaf of bread, but he doesn't remember if bread in French is masculine or feminine. So he asks for three loaves and avoids pronouncing the article, and when the baker brings them out, he says, take back two of them!

When the others started making fun of stuck-up French speakers or anybody else during a break, Potiron just looked at me, meaningfully. He'd sit down on a low-lying tree branch, wolf down his lunch without speaking, and then walk off to smoke a cigarette. He liked good cigarettes, not the kind you bought one at a time that cost next to nothing. His tobacco smelled good, and even though I didn't really like to smoke, I'd wander over his way, over to his long white cigarettes, to his head slightly tipped to the left, with one eye closed, smiling the smile of a satisfied man.

We started talking about the work that never seemed to get done, the materials that hadn't shown up yet, the boss who couldn't tell us when we'd get the extractor we needed to grade the ground, now that the rocks had been removed.

I'm the one who asked if he knew how unions worked.

He looked nervous. "Why're you asking me about that?"

"Because a friend talked to me about unions, but ours, the one for construction workers, well, he doesn't belong to that one. I don't know anybody who does, but I think maybe you do. And I trust you, don't know why."

He was silent, and we got back to work, but one day, after we'd finished, he came over to talk to me: "There's a meeting tonight, if you want, but it's in La Pointe."

I worked things out with Julien so he'd drive me there after he fed his animals.

I was worried because in our part of Grande-Terre, the unions had already run into a lot of problems with bosses and gendarmes. I didn't know all the details, but my father always said that in Guadeloupe every time the little guy asked for his rights, somebody got killed.

I talked to Julien about it. I asked him if things had changed, and he answered that with people like that, you just never knew, and then he thought about it and added he didn't think it could keep on like this forever. Maybe he was trying to reassure me: "If we don't do something, nothing will ever get done, and everything will go on the same as before."

I was ready to believe him. Because with old Absalon—and we'd been trying to change things for the last ten years—I always felt that as soon as we managed to get something out of him, we took ten steps backwards.

※

I really liked going to that meeting, even if I had a lot of trouble getting home and had to walk most of the way in the dark. All the same, it was nice to be alone, like that, at night, to have done something different with my evening, instead of hanging out in the shop on Mayoute listening to pointless discussions.

I thought about everything that'd been said. I didn't ever want to feel sorry for myself, but I realized we were all in the same boat—so little pay for what we did, not even enough to eat, when you thought about how hard the work was and how strong we had to be.

I learned how many workers had been injured in bulldozer accidents. At Absalon's work sites, we hadn't had any problems with equipment, but I'll never forget the driver who was killed on the road and the fact that Absalon had no insurance. I don't know how it finally ended up. But that day all the work buddies went to the site of the accident and the boss was there crying like a baby, crying for that guy who died so stupidly, just because some bastard hadn't stopped at the stop sign.

Of course, he was also crying because he already had plenty of trouble, and that accident was only going to make things harder for him.

I remembered I felt a little ashamed because I was worried they might take the work sites away from Absalon.

My life was connected to his like a button to a buttonhole. I don't know why, but in those days it didn't even occur to me that I could look for another boss. Why was that?

Why do we act like they're part of our family when we know they never ever think of us that way? Maybe because we're a real small country.

I don't understand how I could have thought like that back then. I tell myself I was just ignorant. But after the union meeting, I decided to change. And changing meant leaving the edge of the sidewalk where I usually stood at a distance, watching what was happening from afar, hoping that whatever happened, it wouldn't really touch me. The way you pray that a hurricane that's already torn through the entire ocean and looks like it's fixed to end up right at your doorstep takes a turn at the last minute and hits the island next to you.

7.

Elizabeth pipes up again, "We want to see our teacher."

The principal is surprised because we can hear from Elizabeth's tone that she's not joking around. "Simion, go to my office this instant!"

Annie moves over to Elizabeth and says, "She won't go to your office because we are all waiting for Madame Ladal. If she goes to your office, we all go."

Sonia Zakarius takes it from there: "We are Madame Ladal's students, not students of Madame Desravins, or Madame Laurent, or Madame Limon, or Madame Kancel, or Madame Simet-Lutin. We want to stay together and we want our teacher, Madame Ladal. She told us she'd see us on Friday."

I don't know who says the next thing: "People like to think they can do what they want with us because we're children!"

The principal jumps at that one: "Who said that? Who said that? Nobody dares answer? Well, let me tell you, you *are* just children and you are students in this school and *I* am the principal."

The same voice lashes out (I'm sure now it's Suzy Foggéa), "And just what kind of principal do you think you are?"

We're all real angry and the principal doesn't understand that she'll never be able to calm us down.

"That's enough. I'm calling your parents."

Elizabeth yells she shouldn't bother because we want to leave right now, because we won't go with any other teacher—they're all bad—and because nobody in our class likes wicked stepmothers!

To keep us in school and get us to calm down, she makes us go up to our classroom and sends in the concierge, Madame Parize, to watch us. Madame Parize tries to talk to us, "Children, I know you're disappointed, but the principal is trying to find the right solution."

We don't speak to her and keep our arms crossed over our chests until eleven o'clock.

You can hear a pin drop, as Madame Ladal would have said.

8.

Friday, May 26, 1967. I left my house early in the morning. I left knowing I wasn't going to lean against a tree like a big sad bird and wait for the car horn bellowing like an insult, saying to everybody who's still sleeping: *Here I am to pick up my worker, just like a piece of charcoal left on a rickety table.*

Sometimes I felt that's what I really was: a piece of charcoal or maybe a sack of potatoes, and somebody just places a pickax, a shovel, a pick, or a trowel between the sack's hands and yells to the potato to get going: *"An nou ay: patate, mété'w o travay!"*

That morning I was already up and moving while lots of houses still had their eyes shut. There was a small light here or there; a voice whispering so as not to make a scene and wake up the neighbors, but angry all the same; a child having trouble getting up; a little girl who's wet her *cabanes* again and somebody's going to have to hang the sheets outside so they dry.

I took advantage of the early morning freshness like a man who's finally opened his chest to the winds of freedom and breathed in all he can.

I waited for Léogane's green bus, but it never came, so I hopped on Palatin's old communal mini, the one with the torn seats. *"Ou avè nous jòdla, Guy-Albè?"*

I sat right behind the driver and told him exactly

where I was going, and I spoke my piece like I'd never dared to before: about work, about the humiliation of it, about having to kiss the boss's ass. And the whole bus listened to me, some voices shouting in approval, "That's right! Right on. You're right, you sure are."

Somebody else said, "But be careful, fellas, be careful all the same."

The old ways—the ones I'd lived with since my father told me I had to help out at home, find a job, and keep it—the old ways had started to work their magic on the bus. I knew people here and there were falling back into their old habits, and if I didn't pay attention, I'd fall back into them too: being careful, having patience, staying hopeful, your day will come, don't count your chickens, no plans, no dreams, don't speak too loudly . . . I don't know what came over me, but I kept on talking, more and more, whistling like a bird trying to tell all of creation that he's up and awake—awake like never before.

I said we'd been careful long enough; we'd discussed enough; waited long enough for those men to listen to us, to give us what we'd asked for.

"It's time. The time has come to speak loud and clear. Even *they* know we can't go on like this, but it's like they're incapable of saying, 'Okay, the men are asking for a raise. Let's look and try to see what we can give them.' No, they wait; they pretend they don't give a damn; and they've started to act like they only need to listen to us when we scare them, when their work sites are stopped, when their factories go dead, when their buses don't leave the garage—but, if they'd only think about it, they'd see that they lose more that way than they would if they just tried talking to us. How many times have I seen that—with my current boss and even with the first boss I ever had.

"He ran an even smaller operation, but he really made me feel like I was nothing: told me I was a dumbass, that I didn't understand a thing, that I'd never amount to anything, that it was only because he pitied my family—who he knew—that he agreed to keep me on. And with him, too, a salary that amounted to a hill of beans, but the hours we worked were endless. You had to stay till you finished the job. Like Papa always said, '*Pa ay trapé bab é patron aw, ti gason!*'

"I took it and took it and took it. But now the union has proposed an action and we've decided to go for it—two percent more. Two percent! That's the raise we want and this time we're not treading lightly. Since yesterday, they know we mean business. Since yesterday, we've rallied the troops. And at the first blast of the trumpet, every construction worker—on every work site, in all the forgotten corners of this country, on all the big roads, on all the buildings under construction—at that first note, they heard us say, 'Men, today, we stop! Throw down your shovels, pickaxes, picks, trowels, and hammers. We're stopping work.' You should've heard those guys. Everybody's ready and with us. So today, I know I'm going to speak to my boss and ask the same from all the bosses. Yes, I am! Two percent! And that's not all I'm going to demand. And it's not just me—there'll be maybe ten, maybe a hundred, maybe a thousand. We'll just see."

After that, nobody said a word. The bus continued along in complete silence—a little cough now and again, maybe somebody clearing his throat, or a deep sigh. But I was already far away. I was at La Place de la Victoire, in front of the subprefecture, where we were supposed to meet while we waited for the negotiations to begin.

So I'd left the bus, my ideas had flown straight into the stratosphere, and there was complete silence around me, until a little later when a woman got on with her baskets. The conductor hitched the baskets to the roof and when the woman got her breath back and noticed that nobody was talking, she asked loudly in the strident tone she used to attract clients to her wares: "*Ka ki tini, zò ka véyé on mò isidan?*"

No, nobody had died; this wasn't a wake. We all laughed, even me. It did us good. We were upbeat again, and nobody said anything else serious.

Strange as it seems, I asked the driver to drop me off in front of the boss's house. I really don't know why. It was on the way; I could take rue Vatable until Lethière and end up right behind the subprefecture. I was early; I'd started off before I needed to, out of habit. That habit of getting ready at daybreak when we weren't really meeting up until 10:00 a.m. But what should I have done? Stayed at home, watching my wife get more and more anxious? Watch the kids leave without knowing when I'd see them again, or even if I'd see them again?

As worried as I was, and it was pretty much eating me from the inside, nothing was going to keep me from taking the bus, demonstrating next to Potiron and maybe Julien, closing ranks with other construction guys I knew from different sites, shaking their hands, and then sticking mine in my pockets like a guy solidly planted on his own two feet, a guy who wasn't afraid of a scuffle.

And that's exactly what I did when the bus let me off in front of Absalon's house. I put my hands in my pockets, and if the boss had been on his balcony, he would've seen me look him straight in the eye. But he wasn't there and the house was still closed up. Sand and gravel were piled high on his sidewalk, the water hose was slung across the sand like a sleeping snake, and the wheelbarrow—well, they hadn't even bothered to bring it inside.

Even the boss was neglecting his work sites!

I kept on my way and walked down rue Vatable. The barbers had begun to open their big doors; the smell of warm bread was wafting from Delbourt's Bakery; the popsicle seller was arranging his stock of lemon ice bars; the street sweepers were collecting garbage from the dirty water of the gutters. The town of Pointe-à-Pitre was waking up. I'd rarely seen it so early in the morning.

Passing behind the subprefecture, I saw that the gendarmes had gathered, ready to protect the building. Yep, there they were. I took a good look as I was passing by to gauge how calm I could keep myself, stop my heart from beating so hard. I wanted to see if the old fear was still there, or if the new language pouring out of my mouth had also bolstered my courage. It didn't feel like my heart was doing a flip flop. I walked past, and they didn't pay any attention to me. I could see La Place from the small straight corridor of rue Lethière. It was still too early, and hardly anybody was there.

The sun made its way up into the sky and the kids started to cross La Place, going in all directions, towards Dubouchage, Michelet, Carnot—boys and girls walking gaily to their schools. I hoped they'd go far enough in their studies to not find themselves at the mercy of others, never having learned how to defend their interests. I smiled when I saw the littlest Absalon walk by, a girl who liked to tell stories in front of her mirror while us workers passed each other buckets of cement to finish the second floor. A funny kid who'd sometimes watch us work and swipe our tools for the games she thought up with her brother. We had to fight with them to keep them from taking the wheelbarrow. Maybe they're the real reason the wheelbarrow's still outside. Forgot to put it back in the courtyard. She sure was jolly that morning, that little one. One of her friends was running after her, yelling, "Wait for me, come on, wait!" And her? I couldn't tell what she was saying, but she was repeating the same odd words, laughing and singing. Yeah, she's a funny little bird.

Nothing much happened that morning. We just waited on La Place while negotiations went on at the Chamber of Commerce—some discussion, a run to the bar to wet our throats. Potiron and I stuck together. We wondered what was going on inside, and how come nobody was coming out to tell us what was happening. The delegates had promised to keep us informed about the proceedings, but up till then, nothing.

Over in a corner, near the basketball courts, a group of young men seemed to be waiting too, like us. They were talking among themselves and they weren't leaving La Place. At one point, one of them came over and asked Potiron for a light. I stepped in to try and find out if he worked construction. He just laughed. "Us? We're unemployed, comrade." And he walked away.

9.

When she has to go down to ring the school bell at 11:00 a.m., Madame Parize makes us go with her.

I linger behind to ask if she knows where our teacher is, and she tells me they'd summoned Madame Ladal to the rectory yesterday. But she doesn't know why.

"Will she be back this afternoon?"

"They were going to make up their minds at the education division this morning. I think the principal's already called them. I don't know what they said, but maybe she'll be back—*Sé timoun-la, zò ay tibwen fò!* Behave, children!—I hope so, you have a very nice teacher. I like Madame Ladal. I like her a lot."

Now and then, the principal tries to grab one of us, but we all manage to skip out of the schoolyard.

We end up in the Darse neighborhood, next to the fishmongers and vegetable sellers. We regroup on the corner before crossing rue Duplessis.

Suzy Foggéa slams her book bag on the ground and asks, "What do we do now? *Ka nous ka fè sé timoun-là?*"

Elizabeth thinks we should go to our teacher's house. I really want to do that, but I tell them if we do, the principal will think Madame Ladal put us up to it, and she'll have even more problems with the administration.

I also tell them what the concierge told me, and Tanya protests, "She won't be back. *I pé ké déviré ankò.* She'll never come back to us."

You can feel the terror in her voice! It breaks our hearts. We don't know what to do.

So I think about you, Papa.

I think maybe you could go talk to the school. You're always talking to administrations, to bureaucracies. Why aren't you here now, Papa, when we need you most?

I remember the day Emmett threw a fit. He was threatening to kill the gentleman you gave our dog to because he barked too much. Emmett broke everything in his room. You started to be worried for the man and you felt bad for Emmett so you brought the dog back.

Without really thinking, I tear my dress and break my glasses in anger; and I hope you'll be home to see what I've done.

But no, you're still not there.

No, you don't have lunch with us. And I've promised my friends you'll do something and because they don't have any solutions either—and you don't know this because you're still not home—we're thirty-two little girls depending on you, my Papa, to help.

I leave home after lunch to get back to school by one o'clock.

I'm ashamed to return without anything to say, no good news to tell my classmates.

I'm so ashamed I don't actually go to school.

I hide my book bag in an alley so nobody will ask me why I'm not in class.

I roam around La Place de la Victoire, but I make myself invisible so if I run into a neighbor, she won't go tell you (and she would) that I'm playing hooky.

I watch the market ladies gather their wares, their baskets. I see the bicycle porters coming to pick them up, loading the vegetables they didn't sell. I see the fish-mongers throw seawater on the sidewalks to clean up the traces of fish blood.

And all of a sudden, I hear voices getting louder and louder, voices of people who're really angry. They're yelling something I can't understand.

The market ladies are afraid. They grab everything that's left and take off running. The ones who don't have their own porter will take a bus home.

I hear somebody say that already this morning policemen have beat up some workers.

Someone screams, "If they go after us this after-noon, all hell's gonna break loose! *O swè la, si yo frapé, sa ké chofé alè!*"

10.

What the delegation told us at the afternoon break, around 12:30 p.m., didn't make us feel better—not one bit.

Nothing important had been decided; the bosses couldn't agree on anything. But the main thing to hold on to was we weren't getting anything we asked for.

Some of us yelled to the delegates that they had to go back to the negotiating table and force those men to give us the raise we'd demanded.

Were those guys trying to stall, making us lose even more workdays, just to refuse to pay us? Were they trying to force us into starvation so we'd have to go back to their work sites, humiliated? Did they think we were totally ruled by our stomachs? No, we wouldn't give up! Anger started coursing through our bodies, through our already hoarse voices, spreading silently and more dangerously through the men who were silently pacing nearby, who weren't afraid of anything.

The delegates were able to calm us down some. The meeting with the bosses wasn't over yet; it didn't do anybody any good to get so worked up; you had to understand what they were proposing, think it over, analyze it to see exactly what they were trying to accomplish.

There'd soon be a meeting at union headquarters; people who wanted to go could leave right now, eat somewhere in town.

Somebody yelled, "Eat? With what?"

But we left all the same, went to the docks along the Darse or into the crooked streets around La Place. I was by myself; Potiron had gone straight to headquarters. All I bought was a fistful of cod beignets wrapped in paper. The woman selling the fritters said we shouldn't go looking for death from those bosses. What was she saying? Things were pretty calm.

While I was eating my beignets on a bench on La Place, I spied the boy who talked to Potiron and me that morning. He sat down next to me. He was really very young, maybe sixteen or seventeen.

"Those white guys—they're gonna walk all over you. You won't get a thing. Negotiate, march, demonstrate in the streets, you've done all that. It's not enough anymore."

I didn't say anything.

"You're on our territory here. This is our place. We're here all day long, all evening too. We don't have anything else to do. And we don't intend to work on the docks, being porters, masons—those shitty jobs that are the only ones guys like us can get. It has to stop."

I knew what he was talking about, but I was also wondering how he got by if he didn't work and spent all his time on a bench on La Place.

"Don't you have family, boy?"

"If I didn't have family, I'd be eating wind, *boug an mwen*."

It took me back to the time I lived with my parents, like him; those early days when I didn't have a job, days filled with tension between my family and myself, days when I got up and tried to run away from my mother's sadness, my father's bad mood. I found a way to get all the way out to Gosier, going through Grands-Fonds. I needed to be far from everything I knew. I didn't want to be a pig farmer.

Working the land? Not for me, never. Get out of that; get away from everything! In Gosier I could look at the sea, but even there I wondered what kind of horizon I could have, where my exit was.

My only answer was to return home at noon to my mother's sarcasm: "You always manage to come home just in time for lunch."

Luckily, I hardly ever saw my father. Or we would have killed each other in that house. So, yeah, the trowel, cement, bricklaying, construction sites—that's all that was left at the end of three months spent in total confusion.

I didn't know where to direct my anger, except towards the people I loved most—my mother, father, little sister. And even though I've managed to get married, build a good house with a tin roof with my father's help and the neighbors' too, and had a pretty little girl I'm crazy about, the anger has never really gone away.

But I didn't tell that kid I understood what he was saying; I didn't confide I was hoping we could resolve things, get what we'd asked for, without violence; I didn't tell him I was afraid. I just sat calmly on that bench, squeezing my cold beignets to get some of the oil out, ready to eat them—despite having completely lost my appetite.

＊

I didn't see the kids leave school, but I heard them come back and it got me thinking: Okay, this is it. It's 1:00 p.m., time for negotiations to start up again. The children will study as they always do and then they'll go home tonight, but at the end of the day, something will have changed.

Watching the little kids pass by somberly in the afternoon sun, knowing they were so close, well, it was like they were protecting us. There was no way a prefect would give orders to fire on workers so close to a school, so close to little children.

I couldn't even imagine the idea; it was absurd, vile.

We started waiting again, and the sun shone down on us even more brutally—that hot afternoon Lenten sun. The groups hanging around grew steadily bigger and bigger. It looked like the guys who'd finished work had joined in.

Potiron was back on La Place, and he came over to me. He whispered, "It looks bad, real bad. Seems like those men want to play hardball. Give us nothing. They're just offering crumbs, and I heard one of them said we'd go back to work when we were hungry enough. That's what they always say. Always. Why should we be surprised?"

Me, too, I'd gone back to work for Absalon because I had to take care of my family, even though I'd wanted to see if I couldn't be hired by someone else. I gave in to my wife and to my own fear, the fear I'd ingested with mother's milk, the fear my father gave me as an inheritance, the fear that leaves us with so many sayings, expressions, and proverbs, like "You can't trust another nigger"—the worst fear of all, the one that enrages you, leaves you gasping for air.

That's the rage that suddenly swept through town, the rage the kid on the bench had made me feel. The same rage that launched the stones, the bottles, the conch shells—everything the boys hanging out at La Place had stockpiled there.

I threw stones as well, my arm moving up and down. And before I knew it—I didn't even know why or when—things exploded.

The gendarmes were ready for it. It hadn't taken much time for them to get to the Chamber of Commerce, to guard the building, to guarantee the safety of the men who went to ground inside or those they evacuated like an army of sick chickens dropping green shit behind them. Their guts must have turned to jelly: the negroes were revolting, a revolt from the beginning of time, a revolt they understood as much as we did—those confronting us and those like my boss, wedged in between, trying to keep the hate and fury coming from both sides at bay. So much hate, so much fury we couldn't talk—just simply talk and convince each other to come to some kind of fair solution to address the needs of some and the obligations of others.

The gendarmes were getting into formation when I saw the little Absalon girl slip into an alleyway. A door opened and an old lady let her in. What was that child doing there? I couldn't worry about it; at least she'd found shelter.

I continued to throw stones, breathed in the tear gas they'd unleashed on us. They'd moved back some, and we moved back as well.

11.

The market ladies must know something terrible is about to happen. The ones who manage to take off are in such a hurry they leave fruits and vegetables behind.

I don't know why everybody is scrambling, walking so quickly, speaking so loudly. That's what scares me: I don't know why people are running and where I'm supposed to run to.

When I look over my shoulder, at La Place, I see a lot of policemen. I mean, they look like police because they're wearing blue, but they have shorts like gendarmes and helmets like soldiers.

Everybody rushing past me asks what a little girl is doing there: "*Ka timoun-lasa ka fè la?*"

That's exactly what my brothers and sisters say when they think I'm misbehaving.

But I want to see; I want to understand what's going on. I'm wondering if you're still there, Papa, if you're with the ones running to hide, with those who're screaming about how everything's going to hell, or in the group trying to leave the meeting, the one they talked about on the radio this afternoon, a group protected by the police.

Some boys are throwing stones and bottles. The gendarmes are hurling little bombs. They make a dull noise and release smoke that burns my eyes.

"Gaz! Gaz! Lakrimo!"

I don't know what it is, but it sure stings my nose, eyes, and throat! I run into the narrow alley where I hid my book bag, and an old lady yells at me, "Get out of here!"

Can't she see all the commotion on La Place? I tell her I have no other place to go.

I know I'm being rude, I do know, and the old lady seems to understand how scared I am. I calm myself down and tell her I'm okay, but that I'm going to stay with her until the gendarmes go away.

12.

Everything went to hell at once; the shots stunned us.

"They're firing; they want to kill us."

"*Yo ka tifé fizi! Yo vé depann nou!*"

A body collapsed right next to me, a body whose movements I'd been seeing in flashes, the same gestures as mine: bend over, pick up, throw, shove aside the smoking casings falling in front of us.

I was afraid it was Potiron—I hadn't seen him for a while—but it wasn't him.

That body just crumpled. He was bleeding; his eyes had rolled back in his head, and he was looking at me, stupefied.

I had to get him out of there. A complete stranger who just happened to be next to me and who I had to try to pull out of an ambush.

Some gendarmes were backed up in front of the Chamber of Commerce, others on La Place de la Victoire in front of the subprefecture; others chasing men who were running away towards the Dubouchage School, probably trying to get to Carénage.

I didn't know where to take the wounded guy.

A few fishermen were watching the events unfold from their boats, looking on in disbelief.

I think it was one of them who pointed to a transporter whose delivery cart was loaded with vegetables, probably the husband of one of the vendors who'd come to pick her up. We hauled the guy onto the seat, and the driver, a good man even if scared out of his mind, took off in the direction of rue Duplessis and the Ricou Hospital.

I watched them leave and went back to La Place.

The fighting kept up forever. I lost track of time. There were only shots, screams, stones flying in every direction.

The men who were fighting the gendarmes had no intention of quitting. The gendarmes were certainly not going to stop; they had their orders.

I saw the kid I'd talked to, saw him fall, killed by a bullet right to the head, and I understood we were no match for them: bare hands facing firearms and trained military men.

So I headed up rue Bébian, which would take me to Chemin des Petites Abymes. I wanted to make sure the Absalon kid got home safe. I was worried about her. I hadn't seen her leave that house, a kind of modest cottage on rue Bébian. I wasn't alone in the street: people were talking everywhere, out of breath, running; they were talking about what they'd seen. All over town word was circulating, even reaching the outer districts, so that people who hadn't left their houses would eventually hear that an enormous bullet, larger than anyone around here had ever seen, had blown open the leg of a quiet and easygoing man everybody knew. He'd fought in Algeria, had been in the war, and defended the French flag and France's honor—a country that, in Guadeloupe, now only had blood on its hands. Another guy had been killed on rue Frébault, but nobody knew him. Maybe he came from another township. They described him: a redhead with green eyes and bushy hair. The stories of children were mixed in with the stories of men who'd taken shelter in the Michelet High School, but who'd been chased out by panicked teachers. "Must have been whites," some angry voices shouted, or "half whites," others said. And people showed their colors, frankly and brutally: "The whites killed the blacks, well now the blacks will kill the whites."

"*Blan tchouyé nég, nég ké tchouyé blan.*"

Urgency, fear, anger, vengeance—everything I'd felt when I'd been throwing stones, bottles, and conch shells was being felt by a lot of other people.

I found the spot where I'd seen the little girl enter the cottage and called out her family name, "Absalon! Absalon!" I didn't even know her first name. There were so many of those kids; their names all sounded the same.

The old lady opened the door and I yelled, "Where's the child? I want to take her home."

The kid recognized me and started screaming, probably because I was covered in blood. But I reassured her, "Come on, look here, I'm taking off the shirt and I'll bring you to your house. We're going to go by the back way. You'll hold my hand and we'll get through, as if everything that's happening has nothing to do with us. You understand?"

She said okay.

She wasn't afraid.

The gendarmes had moved towards the center of town, to rue Frébault and rue de Nozières, so we crossed in front of her school and took all the little alleyways between houses, paths I knew like the back of my hand. We cut through courtyards; some streets were calm, completely free of the turmoil that had taken over downtown.

We hurried down a road close to Massabielle Church, a little sloping path paved with stones. I could tell from how she was holding my hand she was scared. Several times, I had to carry her in my arms to get us through a difficult patch, but she held on tight. Like she was my own little one.

We made it to a narrow passage next to Delbourt Bakery on rue Vatable and that's when she said to me, "We're here. That's Mademoiselle Potrizel's school."

And it was true. We were only a few meters from the boss's house. The entrance was shut. I rang. Madame Emmanuel came out and opened the door.

When she recognized me, bare chested and sweaty, and she saw her little girl holding my hand, she paled and started to shake, but I was able to reassure her.

We went in. Her brother, Émile, had made it home from Carnot High School and had told his mother what was happening in town.

I washed up a little. Madame Emmanuel loaned me one of the boss's shirts, and I left to find a bus to take me back to the countryside, far from this insanity. There was no point trying to find anyone else now. Now was a time to lie low.

13.

The old lady lets me in.

She doesn't have a balcony; her room looks onto a courtyard paved with white stones. Limestone. (Right, Papa?)

We sit down in her room and wait together.

She murmurs, "I heard a mess of noise, but I didn't even know what it was. What's going on? Have they decided to wipe out our race?"

I answer that it's because of the construction workers' strike, and I tell her that even my papa's workers didn't come to work on Thursday.

"Oh my child, I don't know anything! I never even leave this house. Where do your parents live?"

"Near rue Vatable."

"How will you ever get home? You can't go through La Place, if that's where people are fighting. You'll have to take rue Frébault and boulevard Chanzy, but you can stay here, and when things calm down, you can go."

"I don't want to be outside when it's nighttime. I want to go home to my Mama this afternoon. She's going to worry."

We wait a long time and the old lady's very nervous.

When it seems to have quieted down outside, I get ready to leave, but I hear a voice yelling my name, "Absalon, Absalon!"

The lady and I are afraid to open the door, but finally she thinks if somebody knows my name, he must know my parents and he can take me to them.

When she opens the door, we see a man covered in blood. Both of us scream, but then I recognize one of my father's workers. It's the one who came and took our radio, who threatened to kill Papa. But I remember that Emmy and Émélie said it had all been cleared up. Maybe he's not mad at Papa anymore and he'll take me home.

He's talking quietly, trying to calm us down.

"Look, I'm taking off the shirt and I'll take you to your parents. We'll go the back way. Give me your hand and we'll just walk on, as if everything that's happening has nothing to do with us. You understand?"

I say okay. I'm afraid of him, afraid of running into gendarmes, but I really want to go home.

He takes a lot of little paths I've never seen before and brings me to Mama, who was already worried because at my school they told Émile I hadn't come back for the afternoon.

Mama hugs me close and I cry a little.

"They're going to kill everybody, Mama. They're going to kill everybody."

14.

It's my turn, me, Justin. I insist on taking the floor before we finish this story. There's no way Guy-Albert should be the only person to speak in this figure! To begin with, I'm the child's uncle. But more importantly, I represent the recent dead: the ones killed today.

A stray bullet, right in my gut. Dead almost immediately, no fuss.

At the point where I felt life definitively leaving my body, what I remembered was shame, and my father, who died of apoplexy.

I saw flashing by me the time I worked the way my father wanted, until a kind of implosion carried him away.

I should have been focusing on the moment, held on to life, screamed no, I won't die without holding my new baby once in my arms, my eleventh, but the first one I want to dedicate myself completely to. Instead of that, I saw the offices, the cane fields, the Baillif Distillery where I had my first job, right up till that god-awful business—that man whose body was partially chewed up in the machines, a man drained of his own blood.

There I was in my role of docile assistant accountant, responsible for paying the widow just what the man had earned for the month he hadn't completed, and not a cent more, nothing to take care of his family's future.

The boss saying, "Justin, we're paying for the casket, that's already enough."

I remember how the head accountant laughed, "Don't bother to buy an oak one. He won't be able to appreciate it."

I smiled, in on the joke.

The first step towards becoming a collaborator, an informant, a snitch, is that complicit smile. Listen to your Uncle Justin, Émilienne! The first step is that little laugh that permits injustice to persist; it's how you look away instead of protesting.

I did that, looked away, hands clenched behind my back, mouth shut, anger controlled behind a smile. A smile that made me deathly ill—stomachaches, vomiting. I guess I've always had a weak stomach.

How could I have smiled at that?

I've lived with shame ever since. I finally pretended to have an allergy attack, to be susceptible to the pieces of cane that escape into the air when the crop is burned. I showed the red patches on my fragile skin. (I'm a redhead after all.) And I quit that job.

Well that's not quite the truth. Maybe I should set the record straight to give myself some credit.

This is how it happened.

A small dark room, the head accountant's desk to the left, surrounded by dockets, me next to the wall, in shadow, a shutter right over my head, letting in a feeble light, dust trembling in its rays. I feel like I'm being smothered, especially since I have to report to the head accountant at least ten times a day.

But that day, he says, "Justin, bring me the order

form, you know, the order for that guy's casket, what's his name—Jazaron."

I had a rebuttal right on the tip of my tongue. It was ready to take off, find its mark, cut through the bullshit, but finally, I smiled, and brought him the order.

I'd already had my revenge: I'd selected a casket in padded mahogany, with a Parma lace lining, four silver handles, a frame for the photo of the deceased. I'd hired six bearers and a hearse. It had purple ropes that the solemn bearers would hold on to with all the respect they'd bestow upon the hand of the dearly departed comrade. I'd already paid for a mass on the fortieth day after his death and for a memorial service whenever the family thought it appropriate.

"Justin, I thought we'd agreed. You were supposed to choose the cheapest casket. Mahogany! What were you thinking?"

I thought I could smell the dead man right over our heads. A crushed, bloody hand waved at me, and then I heard the laugh. Incredible, totally communicative, an explosion of joy in that stifling office. So I laughed too. I grabbed the head accountant and began to waltz with him, repeating, "Mahogany, Justin, what were you thinking?" And then I stopped and pushed him against the wall with one hand while I grabbed the papers he was supposed to sign. He signed. He signed his sarcasm on the funeral bill. Accounting registers tumbled to the floor, dust was flying, a painting fell off the wall and its glass broke—if we can call a reproduction of a five-thousand-franc note with its exotic woman in madras and all those satisfied sugarcane cutters a "painting."

Yep, with the broken glass and the false bank note on the floor, he signed. He even agreed when I told him he was not to open his big mouth to anyone, not to complain to the gendarmes, not a word, otherwise . . . It was after that incident that my father got involved: "He's my son, I've come to ask you to hire him. He's an accountant."

So I left sugarcane for bananas. I don't think I was any better off. In any case, I couldn't rid myself of my shame.

Maybe a stray bullet will earn me forgiveness.

So, my darling favorite niece, would you please tell them to dress me in my blue suit before they bury me? A beautiful blue suit. I want to hear them say how great I look in my coffin, especially your mother.

"He's handsome, don't you think? Don't you think my brother's handsome?"

That's how she'll be able to ward off her grief. At least that's what I hope.

I can't seem to get used to my new appearance: stiff and cold. That's not the cheery me, who always had a laugh ready for the family and for you, sweet Émilienne, my inquisitive girl.

Tell them, too, that I don't want any powder. I'd never get used to the saccharine odor, that blend of talc, death, and naphthalene.

I'm not accustomed to being immobile either, but I want to imagine that dark blue suit in all its proud glory, a perfect complement to my eyes, eyes that change from green to yellow, depending on the weather. What do they look like today? And will they keep on changing now that I'm dead? You're so special, you can probably answer that question, right? Can't you?

Tell them to give me a white shirt and a tie as well. It'll be the second time in my life—that's probably the wrong expression. What would you say?

The first time was when I married that woman. If only she'd miss the funeral! Do you think Emma could arrange that? Let her go complain to the heavens elsewhere, and let me lie in peace—if we can think of death as a vacation.

How in God's name did I ever bind myself to that woman? From the very beginning, I hated our life together, in spite of the kids. All ten of them.

Your mother, my older sister, my adored sister, always asked the same question, "How can you hate her so much and still make a baby every year?"

I don't have an answer to that. Nope, no answer. In the beginning, sex was always a contest. We were taking revenge on each other, at least that's how I saw it. There was no love, only a power struggle on both sides. And the cold winds blowing from the Saint Claude Mountains did the rest. She was always too cold in the morning. I warmed her up just before crawling out of bed. And then I put on that short-sleeved light blue shirt and gray slacks—a uniform without the label—and slipped into my sad life, exactly like my father's, any way you looked at it.

I'm angry with myself today for leaving ten orphans in the hands of that idiotic woman. But I don't feel like talking about her. She meant nothing to me when that bullet hit me in the stomach.

A stray bullet. Or better said: an entirely bad luck bullet. There was no reason on earth for me to be hit by a bullet that afternoon. I didn't even know anything was going on in La Pointe. Not a clue.

You could probably even say it was fate, when you know how much I hate the town of Pointe-à-Pitre. I detest those long flat streets. I'm used to living in the mountains.

In my town, Basse-Terre, it's only a little ways to get from the port to the heights. From where the boulevard Félix Éboué starts to climb and the dank old prison is located, the heights already begin to overshadow the sea. But the noise and smells of Pointe-à-Pitre make me sick. I need the fresh air of my native Basse-Terre, of Gourbeyre where I was a child, of Saint-Claude where I've been living lately—until now.

I only went to Pointe-à-Pitre when I had to, and also to see my beloved sister.

And I had to go on May 26, 1967.

Mother's Day was coming that Sunday, May 28, but celebrating it was out of the question! The shrew was just waiting for it, so she could go and boast in the streets, "He still belongs to me. That other one can take a hike, the one who says she's pregnant by him. Because I'm the one he offers presents to on Mother's Day. I'm the mother of his children."

I knew her routine too well to get caught in that trap. But May 28 is also my little Georgia's birthday, and I'd promised her a pair of jeans. She likes to think of herself as a cowboy. She has such great fun with her brothers. They perform scenes from cowboy movies they go see at

Le d'Arbaud on Sundays, right after mass. It was always fun to watch her draw her two pretend pistols, her feet wide apart, her eyes narrowed as she found her target. She made me laugh. I laughed when she pretended to slide a glass of whisky over the counter of an imaginary bar. But she wanted jeans and all the equipment, a belt with a holster for her pistol, a bullet pouch that could hold twenty-two bullets, a Stetson, and a sheriff's badge shaped like a star. She'd asked for all that for Carnival and I'd laughed, not understanding how it might hurt her. She opted out of the Carnival parade at her school, the first time she wasn't the center of activities at Carnival time. So I swore to myself I'd get her what she wanted for her birthday. I'd gone to La Pointe to buy a belt, a pouch, and a sheriff's star when that bullet ripped open my stomach—without my seeing anything coming, without even having the time to understand what was happening.

If somebody had asked me about the workers' strike, I would no doubt have expressed my disapproval, probably with a little smile, that complicit smirk I mentioned at the beginning of this story. It's crazy, isn't it?

Silence, a smile, and every man for himself—that's me.

I'm not a rebel; things that get to me aren't political, but human, like that business with the casket and the worker from the sugarcane plant. Yeah, I can imagine doing things like that, but I can't imagine striking or building barricades. I really knew nothing about what was happening in La Pointe that day. Not a thing.

I'd never even set foot on La Place de la Victoire,

which is ugly, if you ask me. I'm repeating myself, probably, but honestly not a thing about Pointe-à-Pitre attracts me. I have no attachment to its polluted port or its outlying districts, especially where my sister Emma, her husband Emmanuel, and their children live.

When I get to La Pointe, I have trouble orienting myself, finding it hard to know where it starts and where it ends, wondering how to stop ending up in the township of Abymes. It's so immense, so labyrinthine, there's hardly any space for Pointe-à-Pitre. And that "Peter's Point"—all two square kilometers of it and some change—likes to think of itself as the capital of this country! I know I'm sounding like a bourgeois from Basse-Terre.

Of course we're in competition, especially with the subprefecture lounging on La Place de la Victoire—and just what "victory" could that be? But Basse-Terre is where the real prefecture and the administration of this entire county are located—that is if you want to think there really is something like an administration. But I don't give a damn about these rivalries between prefectures and subprefectures. The reason I don't like La Pointe is simply because it stinks and it has no beautiful views; you can't see the horizon when you're there. It makes me feel sick, boxed in, as if I've been tied to the ground on my stomach, in the middle of all those filthy gutters full of disgusting fish that thrive in dirty water.

When I get to the bus station in Bergevin and make my way through the swarming crowds, I always try to avoid the pools of water in those giant potholes until I get to boulevard Chanzy, which is endless. And when I finally get to rue Frébault, I seek refuge in the stores if there's anything I need to buy. But I rarely buy anything in La Pointe. Usually when I go, it's to see my dear sister, Emma. I need to speak to her, to see her, to listen to what she needs to tell me, to hear her laugh. Sometimes I succeed in making her laugh in the midst of her list of complaints, even if she feels she has to hide her mouth with her hand to not expose the broken teeth marring her beautiful face. She lets herself go with me: we have fun, like we did when we were kids. My sister isn't really happy with her little tailor. I can't imagine calling him anything else—the little tailor—even though he's gone on to do other things. In my mind, he'll always be that. I said so to our mother. I told her Emma shouldn't marry him. I thought he was too old to marry my sister: twenty-eight years old. Emma was only nineteen.

But our mother kept saying it was time to accept a marriage proposal. Had there really been others? I have no idea.

"I'm done with it. There's nothing more I can do for her."

Our mother was only forty-two and already worn out, worn out by work, by poverty. All she wanted was to marry off her daughter and have it done with. I was living with my father, so I wasn't a burden.

"I've had it with responsibility."

But twenty-eight and pretentious . . . "She works; she helps you out," I pleaded.

"Enough is enough, I've already said so."

You couldn't argue with our mother.

But I remember the words she muttered, "A small man, a negro who thinks he's a big boss."

Luckily, the times I slip into my sister's home, as though I were a wily lover, her husband is never there. I don't even know when he's usually at home, when he gets up and leaves, when he comes back. But around two o'clock, I'm sure he won't be there. So my sister and I close ourselves in the kitchen, as far away as we can get from the smell of the animals in their pens at the back of the garden.

I can't stand the smell of chickens, or rabbits, who seem to always want to make faces at me, wiggling their soft rosy noses. And besides, it's cooler in the kitchen. It's in the shade and not too big, just enough for us to sit down on a bench and put our heads together—and we can go on for hours while her husband's away and the kids are in school—and after the girl who helps her with housework has hung up her smell on the back of the kitchen door. During this time, which is ours alone, we talk about our lives.

We also talk about our brother's life at sea; he joined the navy when he was just seventeen.

Timothée wanted to flee the feeling of suspension in Basse-Terre. That's what he said at least. What do you mean by "suspension," we asked him. And he answered by talking about the women who went up and down the hills without appearing to move; it happened so slowly. He talked about how everybody drew out their words, making them last forever. He complained about always meeting the same people in the same place at the same hour. He disliked the passivity and absence of passion that seemed to emanate from Basse-Terre.

If during these last months he'd been able to experience the rush of anger in the streets of Basse-Terre, especially in March, he might have changed his mind. But when he was free of the war against the Germans and panicked at the idea of returning to Basse-Terre to twiddle his thumbs, he elected to plunge into the conflict in Indochina, in Saigon, in a climate even more humid than La Pointe's. It took seventeen days of travel on *Le Pasteur*, but that period of his life cut him off from the rest of the world.

I never told Emma any of his stories of ambushes, deaths, atrocities, Vietnamese prostitutes, or hunting wild black pigs in the jungle. For years after his return, Timothée's life looked normal, even banal—a wife, kids, an okay job at Saint Hyacinthe Hospital. And then he fell into a bottomless depression.

He hasn't spoken for over a year; he just looks at us and cries, his body overcome by sobs, like a child.

The big man—who used to pick up our mother as though she were a feather to tuck her in bed in the last years of her life, who delicately washed her and braided her hair—has turned into a long sack of bones piled into a beige leatherette armchair in a sitting room. And all this in a cramped building, backed against the mountains of Basse-Terre, trapped like a beached ship.

I navigate from one to the other, from Timothée to Emma, from La Pointe to Basse-Terre, and it seems that in 1967 I'll have seesawed from a rioting city to a city in revolt. I won't have had the chance to talk with my sweet sister about the fury taking over La Pointe, because I never made it to her neighborhood. I only heard her voice in my ear, at the moment when death claimed my body, after the bullet tore up my insides. Yes, her voice, as soft as my mother's when she was finally at peace, a voice hovering over me, as if she'd crossed the city to be with me in my last moments. She still doesn't know a bullet has just robbed her of her brother. When will she find out?

I hear my sister's voice and it seems my mother is speaking to me.

In fact, I actually see my mother on the other side, welcoming me and connecting me to other victims of today's violence with one of her old stories.

⁂

One year Mother told us this story about a young man who disguised himself as Death. This took place in Gourbeyre during Carnival.

"Nothing really very scary, children. Just a young boy, hardly more than a child, who covered his head with a sheet. I don't even think he poked holes in it for his eyes. Just a Carnival mask of Death, really nothing more than that. So he walks near the gendarmerie in Gourbeyre and some gendarme's wife, some white lady on her veranda, sees him, gets scared, and runs back into the house screaming. What could she have said? That a black guy tried to touch her, rape her? Whatever it was, her gendarme husband grabbed his pistol without a second thought, and he shot and killed the Carnival ghost, a ghost hiding a very real young man. How can I capture what the population felt then: apathy, frustration? The boy's father had been in Basse-Terre, who knows what he was doing there or why. But when he heard his son had been killed by the gendarmes in Gourbeyre, he decided to walk home and claim his son's body, probably to mourn. Maybe to take revenge. Who can say whether or not he said what any father might—must—say upon learning his child has been murdered: '*Tala ki tchouyé pitit an mwen-la, an ké fin chyé avè'y!*'

"Yeah, maybe he said he'd make the man who killed his son pay, maybe he did. But any father who respects himself has to say such a thing: a son is not a dog— and even a dog, you don't shoot it when it gets its head stuck in a paper bag and runs around like an imbecile. You just laugh. You laugh, right? In any case, the mounted Gourbeyre gendarmes, claiming the father had made his intention to seek revenge clear (even if nobody heard it), arrested him, the man who'd just lost his son. They caught up with him on the road from Basse-Terre and tied him to a horse and dragged him all the way from Basse-Terre to Gourbeyre: trotting, trotting, trotting, galloping, galloping, galloping. And they laughed, those mindless men; they laughed thinking that such a demonstration of strength would shut the population up. They laughed because they were adding another dead man to the family of a dead man. They laughed until the sound of fury jarred them out of their insouciance and their arrogance.

"The sound of fury is like the sound of the earth. Who here has heard the roar of the earth when it's angry? You can't locate where it's coming from, but when the sound of the earth starts to grow, you understand how you're always living your life on tiptoe and that something greater, totally invisible, has given you permission to scrape by. And so the sound of the people's fury, from Gourbeyre, Basse-Terre, Vieux-Habitants, Bouillante, Capesterre, arose from the corners of the land because our words travel faster than telegrams. Because our words are like the earth's words, like its sound: You've hardly understood how it spreads, how fast it's going, where its epicenter is located before it's caught you off balance, sent you into a tailspin, up-ended cars, burned down buildings, floored men, and torn apart those on the fault line between two worlds. It makes those living in arrogance head for the hills. They hide and don't know where to hide; their guns no longer serve a purpose because all of a sudden people's chests have become like steel, and bullets can't hurt them.

"In no time at all, in all the towns around, men and women, from the oldest to the youngest, had saddled their horses, prodded their donkeys, grabbed their swords, sharpened their knives, broken off enormous branches from mango trees, and resuscitated those old-time whips that had been hidden under what passed for goodwill. But in the wink of an eye, the homicidal gendarme and his wife had been smuggled out and sent away to, I hope, the coldest part of their country. Over there, in the Jura Mountains, where they exiled our great ancestor, Toussaint Louverture—exiled to death. Let every single part of their bodies freeze! Let them starve to death!

"The organized escape only succeeded in making people even angrier. Instead of giving the crowd the ones responsible for the outburst of violence, as scapegoats for what had happened, they chose to evoke The Law—that symbol of power, that ensemble of rules exasperating everybody till the end of time. So lightning struck all the government buildings. The court burned. The prefecture burned. The prison burned. Police headquarters burned. The schools and the factories burned, the cane fields burned. And all the shops of the sellouts and collaborators burned. And the whole town of Basse-Terre and the village of Gourbeyre would have burned, too, if they didn't finally find a negotiator that people believed in and listened to—when the fury started to abate, when people could start seeing each other again, when that thing that can't be named came back into focus. When they began to come to grips with the extent of the damage caused by losing control."

While this story was finishing, I quietly exited La Pointe, accompanied by the last words of my mother's witnessing, words falling gently one after the other into my ears, words attending me even despite the vertigo threatening to overtake me, widening the space between my body and myself.

I left my dirty clothes, my bloody body, my confusion in rue Frébault and said goodbye to my unborn child, who will only ever know me through photographic portraits, those artificial poses struck in local studios.

15.

God of Thunder! What in heaven's name are my poor old ears hearing?

It would've been better if I hadn't come back, dragging my bones around just to witness another earthquake in this country I call mine! Lord help us!

But, I ask you, *tonnèdidyé*, what am I supposed to do with only one leg? Useless to boot! Godammit all to hell!

If the good Lord can't even find it in Him to grant us a little peace, a full stomach, a roof over our heads—the least a person can ask for himself and his descendants—why am I even holding out for a shitty quadrille ball in a phony paradise with angels who don't give a damn. They've seen too much crap year after year! And His Majesty himself won't even raise a finger!

Yeah, it's starting again. Not that it's ever really over.

I try not to think about it, but it's coming back like yesterday.

I tried to bury it when they buried me. All those long sad nights when we watched over the dead, when I went to see families silent as horror itself, real horror, the one that cuts your vocal cords in one quick slice, like a razor.

I can see those long lines around the bodies, people stopping in front of eyes now shut, trying to take it all in. It's the last time, really, the last time they're going to see this boy, going to see how even in death anger lingers in a creased forehead, a pinched mouth—proving that death brings not a bit of the peace we're promised. And underneath the clothes, the last clothes he wore, there's blood, dried blood, wiped clean by the careful hands of the man at the funeral parlor, as smooth as the Tordoncan kid who straightened out my arm that got stuck when I died.

A glance, the sign of the cross, a parade of the defeated—and here's just one more . . . I see those get-togethers where they hold back tears, let nothing show: not pain, anger—nothing. It's like they've accepted it, yet they're still thinking about how to get even, whack the killers—one day, somehow, one way or the other.

They've been taking detours, skirting trouble, for such a long time, but one day it boils over. They'll explode and then go back to life as usual.

Because patience and time accomplish more than force or rage.

Everything in its time. *Tout' cochon ni sanmdi a yo!*

Nobody escapes fate. *Sa ki la pou'w dlo pa'a chayé'y!*

Pass around the proverbs at the communal table! Pass them around; share them. Those ready-made words that help us wait.

Yeah, I see them, those long wakes accompanied by the sounds of the conch in the night, from one hill to the other—our call to prayer—and those slow and dignified burials, the long march of dark colors followed by the scent of clothes just pulled out of storage.

How is it possible we let the little one see what she saw? Who could've imagined the simple dismissal of a teacher would've led to that child bearing witness to such butchery? What do we think will come of all this, this upset born of what seemed like a minor incident in a child's life, an event in the daily routine of some thirty little girls, a tiny incident about nothing at all—at first— but one that spread from room to room, class to class, in a school where rebellion was just around the corner.

A miniscule spark that ends up igniting a powder keg and causing an inferno. We've lit that fire so many times in the streets, in the squares, at the shore, on the roads: barricaded bridges, overturned and burned cars. Shots fired, men arrested and jailed, the dead quietly buried, their bodies disfigured by blows, old men beaten and abandoned in the street like dogs thrown in the garbage in the middle of the night.

A long list of names will only get longer with all those voices crying out, in a country where peace will never come, where it's too dark, where fury smolders on and on. A whole host of voices is emerging from a chasm Émilienne didn't even know existed, but that she's now starting to detect. Now that she's decided she needs to know, to learn, to hear, to ask why such violence reigns, why a woman she and her classmates love so much could be targeted.

So the two fires have come together: the flame of the teacher's disappearance has added to the great blaze of injustice. And what a foolish mistake to have lit that spark—which seemed so harmless—because it will never go out now. And it's made the dead rise up and mix their voices with the living.

What idiot doesn't understand that dry branches always feed a fire? We're a forest of dry branches just waiting for a spark. How can they not understand that, given how long this has been going on?

That forest! That's what her father ought to speak to her about! Why the hell doesn't the bastard come home?

Given everything that's happened in town today, I can't believe that man isn't worrying about what's become of his family, if somebody might be dead or wounded, if the two and a half floors of the unfinished house he cares about so much are still standing.

16.

The chorus? The callers?
What should we name ourselves now? We don't really
know anymore!
We're overwhelmed, and it's coming from all sides.
The voices aren't paying attention to us. The instruments are playing all at once.
The dancing's chaotic.
But we have to hold on for the last figure,
The finale, the last gasp.
Ladies and gentlemen, make way for *pastourelle*!

THE FOURTH FIGURE: *PASTOURELLE*

1.

Friday, May 26, 1967. Our family's scattered all over town.

We don't know where our brothers and sisters are. They should've been home from school by now.

Émile's managed to return from Carnot. His teachers let them leave right away, but there's no news from Emmett or from Émilio, and not a word from Émelie.

Mama's having trouble breathing. She's holding her stomach, like Émelie does when she's upset.

Emmy pulls me into the bathroom and washes me from head to toe. I want to tell her that I know how to wash myself, but I understand she wants to make sure I'm all there.

I feel kind of weak inside, but at the same time I know my heart is hard, hard like the faces of the fishermen I saw in their boats on the Darse—while they were watching the gendarmes on the docks chase those young guys throwing bottles and stones.

I'm afraid for Émelie, Emmett, and Emilio.

I'm afraid for you, Papa, but I don't know what to think about you either. I wonder if you were really there at that meeting, in the middle of that violence.

So I let Emmy wash me. I try to start breathing again without being angry, but I can't.

I don't feel like crying or tearing my dress or scratching my face. It's not me I feel like hitting and scratching.

2.

Standing a few meters from Absalon's house, I was thinking about everything that'd happened that afternoon, how I had one of his shirts on, and I'd shepherded his little girl all across the city and through the rioting.

I was thinking he sure wouldn't have risked his life for me or one of mine. We were on different sides of the fence, like opponents—but maybe I just couldn't manage to see all his family as enemies, adversaries you had to beat no matter what the cost. I thought about the warm little body of his daughter in my arms. That child had never shunned me; she'd played with my tools, followed us around while we worked. She was a strange little kid who didn't talk like other children, who asked all kinds of questions. But I'd never seen in how she looked at me, in how she acted towards me, anything that said she didn't respect me, anything that said she might not even have some affection for me.

I was glad I'd brought her home.

But I wondered what would happen next. Things weren't going to stop just like that.

The gendarmes were probably going after people, arresting them, and putting some in prison, starting with the union guys. I was sure Julien would be one of the major suspects, and even if I trusted him, I was hoping he'd keep his mouth shut. I hoped nobody knew me well enough to find me, however they might try.

I was wondering if when everything calmed down, we'd be able to pick life back up the way it'd been before and whether what had happened would change something between us and the bosses, with the people who really ran things—the ones we hardly ever get a glimpse of, except when we're supposed to fix up their houses when they start to get shabby, or when they need to know how to put up a wall, or when they want to buy cheaper material.

I couldn't see a single bus on the horizon. I'd heard the buses had gone back to their terminal, in the outskirts, in order to keep from being set on fire, from being caught in the same frenzy of wrecked and burned cars that had erupted in Basse-Terre last March.

Thinking about Basse-Terre, the authorities must have known that the rioting would happen again; they must have decided this time they'd be prepared for it. And, yeah, they were ready all right—ready to shoot anything that got in their way.

I was going to have to walk home, to avoid the major roads. I was thinking that when the boss's Dauphine stopped in front of me: "*Guy-Albè, monté.*"

He opened the car door for me. He was serious, very quiet. I'd never seen him like that.

"*Ola ou kay? Ou ka rantré?*"

"*Fo an monté a kaz, patron.*"

"*An ké menné'w, pa ni vwati ankò.*"

That was it, all we said till we got to my place. It was the time I like best, the time of day when the sun has just started to set, one of those moments that makes you calm, like in the early morning, when you can look around without the sun washing everything out. I like this special time when night starts to creep in. I like it too because the animals all seem to have something to say: the birds share their adventures with those coming back to nest and with those getting ready to retire elsewhere for the evening, one last salvo of chirping and cooing—while the cows stretch their necks up to the sky and open their mouths to bid the day farewell. The birds whiz around in all directions, predict rain, change their minds, fly away somewhere else—heading out to the sea you can't detect from here, but you can feel it in the air, in the beautiful light that's ours. So what if it's the only country I know, and only some of it at that—some of Grande-Terre. I love the color of the land, the light, the people.

Sitting at my side, the boss seemed to enjoy the silence. I was wondering where the hell he could've been during the events, if he'd seen the bodies on the ground, the blood in the streets, the anger of the young guys and the men like me. I wondered, too, if he knew I'd brought his daughter home.

It seemed like he was listening to my thoughts because he started to speak, and the man who spoke wasn't the man I knew. The new man's voice caught in his throat; his words came out softly, without the aggression I'd always heard there, and those words said that what had just occurred was a horror. That voice, I understood, had seen dead men on La Place, wounded people in town, men stopped in their tracks while they were running, a father cut down while he was holding his child's hand. That voice had seen bodies hurriedly carted off, men wiped off the face of the earth when they'd done nothing but run some errands; others killed leaving their offices, others leaving school. That voice said that for the last three days, since Wednesday, he'd had a feeling things were about to disintegrate. That voice told me what was said in the places he found himself, where he lurked unnoticed because he kept his mouth shut. What was said there was unbelievably violent, a kind of violence he'd forgotten, either because he was naive or he wanted to believe the past was past and we were headed for new times.

That voice, scratchy, strangled, emotional, said the man who was speaking didn't know why he'd done the things he'd done in his life if it was only to discover he was still right where he'd started. Even if he's a boss, even if he had a house built that proves he's tried to better himself—a house that didn't have a finished roof because he'd intended to build higher and higher—and not just for him but for his kids too. To forget the mud on his heels, the tiny hamlet even smaller than the one we were in; to forget, in that village, a street even narrower than the one we were on; to forget, finally, on that street, a house, a cabin, even smaller than the one we were in front of. A miniscule village, microscopic, incredibly dark, with all the cottages made of dark wood—not a single one painted white, not a single one that looked finished, unprotected wood that in the best case turned grayish under the rain and sun in that infinitely tiny village where he was born. That voice said there was absolutely nothing wonderful about his childhood, a childhood he had to endure, nothing that sang, nothing that spoke to the joy of going to the river for water and all that kind of bullshit you read about in books. No, just a real hard, brutal life—violence, mockery, and cruelty as survival strategies. Mockery was simply a way of devouring others, devouring yourself—chewing on your arms, legs, face, eating yourself so that nobody else could consume you. Faced with such cruelty, the only escape was through bleak comedic relief, dark humor: nothing bothered you because nothing mattered.

That voice said they made fun of his skinny legs, his crooked teeth, his black skin—absolutely black skin, which became a symbol of something very bad in a country where nobody talked about race, where racial hatred wasn't supposed to exist because we'd all been freed; everybody was free, right? Everything depended on where you were in the hierarchy. That man I didn't recognize said he used to laugh a lot, but that each time he laughed he was able to see in the eyes of those around him a profound sadness, as if they were saying, *So that's what you really think of me.* And nowhere did anybody have a thought that would give you hope, push you a little further, help you believe in yourself; no concession to goodness. You had to be the most violent, to hit, punch, pound the table, throw stones, yell, act like a tough guy, test other people all the time.

And the voice continued:

"I'm going to tell you a story that keeps me awake at night, Guy-Albert. My friend Joseph, my sister

Augustine, and I are all around an open fire and Joseph has a spoon in his hand. We watch it get red hot and then, without warning, Joseph grabs the spoon and presses it into Augustine's shoulder. He burns himself, of course, but it hurts less than it does Augustine, whose skin crackles as it burns—less than it hurts me, my gaze burning into him, as I sit there terrified. My sister doesn't budge, as if she had no choice but to take it—not a scream, just a small sound quickly muffled, probably from surprise. She let it happen, no tears in her eyes, no anger, just a kind of furious desire to be stronger than the pain . . . What keeps me from sleeping, Guy-Albert, is trying to understand where Joseph got the idea, why Augustine was so sure she had to accept and submit to that torture."

I suddenly saw those old drawings of slaves being marked by hot irons, those things that happened a long time ago but have stayed with us. All that came back to me, but I didn't speak.

And then the voice added:

"You did the right thing. Nothing, not even a three-floor house, can justify massacring children, brothers, friends because people want a raise of a couple dollars."

He stopped, waiting for what he'd just said to sink in. I was floored by what he'd admitted. We'd need some pretty solid machines, the best tools, to clean up the discussion shaping up in front of us. All the shovels, the pickaxes, the forklifts, the trowels, the sifters—sifters as big as the island itself—to separate out the muddy past. All those tools danced around me, around us, two men seated in a car while night was falling, two builders whose unfinished construction was already starting to crumble.

The boss—but at that moment there wasn't simply a boss and a worker present—Sauveur Emmanuel Absalon started to speak again. He had to go home and face Madame Absalon. Well, he was used to that. What he truly feared was how his little girl would look at him, her questions, how he'd see her change when he told her the truth, how she'd distance herself from him, just like the other children had done, judging him, taking a silent stand against him when he and their mother argued.

He knew the little one had worked herself into such a state that her mother had taken her to his sisters'. His little girl was shaken by his absence.

"Three days away, Guy-Albert. Three days. It's the first time I didn't have the guts to go home to my unfinished house. I feel like tearing it all down. It's the first time I don't have a clue what to say to the children, the first time I won't be able to tell them stories to make them laugh. The first time we won't cry from laughing so hard; the first time they won't wonder why their father cries so easily when he's always said that real men don't cry. You've seen me cry, Guy-Albert, you know. I don't understand why the tears come, all by themselves; I can't control them. They seem to erupt from an endless river that's been running through me for a long time, at least since that spoon seared Augustine's shoulder.

"I'm ashamed of the people I associate with, ashamed of those men with their big equipment who used to come sit in my salon, even if I was proud of my work sites, of the roads we were building. I was proud but at the same time I hated those men. I hated the kick-backs I had to pay them, the bribes to the mayor's office, the jewelry offered to his wife to avoid the scrutiny of the tax collectors, those fake friendships, those miserable games of pinochle—all of it so I could take care of my children. Yours, as well, even if you don't believe I was thinking about them. I'm ashamed of spending time with people who sell their friends, who inform on them, like that principal who turned in Émilienne's teacher, who said she was a dangerous revolutionary, someone who believed in independence and autonomy, someone we had to keep away from our children. She even bragged about bringing up the October 15, 1960, regulation, the one that says: *On the recommendation of the Prefect, and without other formalities, employees of the state and all other public institutions working in overseas departments whose behavior is found to disturb the public order can be immediately called back to metropolitan France by the Minister who heads their division in order to be assigned elsewhere.* Yeah, I can recite it by heart, and it makes me even more ashamed. Ashamed because all I asked was to let the children finish their year with Madame Ladal, knowing how much my little girl loved her. My darling Émilienne could finish the year, and then the principal could inform on Madame Ladal, send her away later, but send her away, all the same. Do you see, Guy-Albert? I'm ashamed not to have had the courage to tell that principal how despicable I thought she was, with that wig she wears because she can't accept her own hair, just like she can't accept being black, and with her obsequious manners—the way she lowers her eyes, bows and scrapes to obey the people she's accepted as her masters. I wasn't brave enough, and now I'll have to face my daughter. She'll have two questions that terrify me: 'Where were you?' 'What's happened to my teacher?'"

When he'd finished talking, I told him that his little girl had been in the streets of La Pointe when the rioting broke out, that I didn't know why or why she wasn't in class then. I told him how I brought her home, reassuring him that after what she'd seen, she'd be far more worried about him than her teacher. And that was that. He could go home now. He'd better go back to his family, because the madness was going to keep up all night long and tomorrow and for a long time after. He'd better take shelter pretty quick. Me too. A little girl was waiting for me as well, not too far from where we were.

3.

They finally all arrive home: Émérite, Emmy, Émelie, Émilie, Emmanuel, Émilio, Emmett, Émile.

Mama grabs each of her children and holds them close; she feels a little better. "Now all we need is your Papa."

My brothers and sisters have come with stories that are a lot worse than mine.

Emmett saw some guy's head blown open and one of the guy's friends hold his brains in his hands, trying to keep his friend alive.

Émilio saw bodies being hauled around in bicycle carts, like dirty bundles of bloody laundry.

Émelie didn't see any dead or wounded, but she knows a lot of people were hit by stray bullets; they're saying tonight will be terrible, that no one should go out because the dogs are loose.

She says that a few times, "The dogs are loose."

We sit down in the courtyard and wait.

Émile asks, "What are we waiting for?"

We're all exhausted. We're so tired, so knocked out, we feel like throwing up. Nobody's able to answer Émile.

Mama goes off to close the hallway door so that nobody will go out again or come in. That's when we hear her cry out.

I think it's you.

A man we don't know is there. He repeats to my big sister Emmy what he's just told Mama: Uncle Justin was killed today, on the street.

"And Papa?"

Nobody answers me. Mama isn't hearing anything anymore.

So I say I'll wait for you, wait all night long if I have to. In the courtyard.

I sit down on Mama's little bench.

I'm still sitting there.

I'm still waiting for you to ring the doorbell.

4.

The time has come to end this quadrille.
It's time for us to accompany the ladies,
Greet the Queen,
One, two, three.
Time to call it a day.
But let's be clear.
We will wait with Émilienne, even if, as she requests, we wait at a distance.
We'll wait, but not just for our father.
We'll wait until someone tells us how our Uncle Justin was killed, why Colette and Julien Ladal have disappeared. We'll wait until someone explains all this to us. To us, too.
We'll wait for the finale of the finale. For the dance to end.

END

A Conversation with Gerty Dambury
by Judith G. Miller ❋ *October 15, 2016*

Judith G. Miller: Your novel depicts centrally the experience of one family's response to the upheavals of May 1967 in Pointe-à-Pitre, the largest city in Guadeloupe. I'd like to start this interview by asking about the context, that is, the refusal of management and business owners to cede to the construction workers' union demands for better pay. As I understand, it went like this: the construction workers strike and demonstrate. The French prefect running things in Guadeloupe calls in not only local police (mostly white guys) but also the French military, and both respond to the strikers with clubs, tear gas, and bullets. This leads to indiscriminate killing. Possibly hundreds of Guadeloupeans lose their lives.

Gerty Dambury: That mostly sums up what happened. There were all kinds of people killed and wounded, people shopping with their families and not at all demonstrating in the part of town where the strike was happening. That shows how really mad the police were! But you know what really interests me about this tragedy is how the event was covered up, as though it never happened. In that sense, it's not unlike what went on after the demonstration by Algerians in Paris in 1961. In that instance, protestors in favor of Algerian independence were also attacked by riot police. A lot of people ended up dead, floating in the Seine. And this terrible violence was also covered up by the French government. We've only recently started to see reporting and statistics on what actually occurred in both cases.

JM: So you write about May 1967 to memorialize it, to make us think about the relationship of former colonies with the centralizing power of France?

GD: Yes, but not just that, because imaginatively recasting May 1967 also allows me to try to capture the complexity of Guadeloupean society at a point when many rural people were pouring into the big city to try to find a way to survive. The sixties were a turning point for Guadeloupe. After World War I and World War II, Guadeloupeans demanded French citizenship. But twenty years after we became a department in 1946, we realized that not much had changed. We were asking in the sixties—and we're still asking— what it means to be French, but not really French.

JM: Is that because of Guadeloupe's status as an overseas department?

GD: That and the fact that France has never come to grips with its own involvement in slavery. In Guadeloupe, the majority black population's still much poorer and less powerful than what's left of the white planter class. These former plantation owners kept their land and even received financial reparations for having "lost their slaves"! Moreover, metropolitan French people still come in to run things. In fact, the entire administration is made up of white French people.

JM: If I've understood things correctly, this project was also a way for you to recover some of your own lost memories.

GD: That's right, because I was only ten years old when it happened, and like the rest of my brothers and sisters (there were eight of us), I'd repressed it. It all came back to me during a conversation with my big brother in the late nineties when we were working on a musical homage for my father. We sat in my brother's kitchen in Switzerland and the memories started to flood in, things we'd never talked about before. He'd seen some of the gruesome incidents I talk about in the novel, and he'd also been dispatched to fetch me home from school on May 26, when everything erupted. We took back alleys to avoid the street battles.

JM: Is this, then, an autobiographical novel? I ask because the main character, Émilienne, around whom everything turns, is nine years old, and the chorus that protects her and helps develop her story is made up of her eight brothers and sisters.

GD: First of all, I did a lot of research on this period, especially after the immense social unrest of 2009, and a lot of what I learned finds its way into the novel. Second, nothing I write is truly autobiographical, but there are bits and pieces of what I've observed all my life in the characters. The father, for example, Sauveur Emmanuel Absalon, is a striver and a small businessperson, like my father was. But he also has the character traits of a couple of my aunts, and of a lot of people I've known. He's cautious, he bows down to the white power structure because he can't bear being humiliated. He's like a dog who's gotten used to being beaten. A dog who hunkers down with its belly to the ground when someone approaches.

JM: That's the opposite of your women characters, at least most of them.

GD: Well, Émilienne, the schoolgirl; Nono, the ninety-eight-year-old ghost who comes back to tell Émilienne about her father; and Madame Ladal, the schoolteacher who's gone missing and who launches Émilienne's quest to understand what's happening, are all fighters. That's for sure. Three generations of women who say no to authority, who resist and put their own lives in danger, who won't be bossed around by the men in their lives.

JM: Even Émilienne's mother resists the petty bullying of the father, at least in her own way.

GD: Yes, she does resist. She's even insolent! But talking about the father: that bully, that guy who goes too fast, who's had no time to think about why he's doing what he's doing, is the character who changes the most. He finally understands what his form of collaboration has led to, and he revolts. He's like what the Martinican writer Édouard Glissant says about Caribbean people in general: "In every person from the Antilles, there's someone who accepts and someone who refuses."

JM: This gutsiness to refuse, to not cooperate with a structure that debases certain people for the benefit of others, characterizes all five "visitors" who come to witness in Émilienne's courtyard as she waits for her father to come home. They help her solve the riddle of her disappeared teacher. The five outside voices create a mosaic, a kaleidoscopic portrait of Guadeloupe.

GD: Yes, and almost all these night visitors are dead and ready to condemn by their own example the ways in which a certain social and political hierarchy has truncated their existence.

JM: Hilaire, for example, once a neighbor, has taken his own life because of how another neighbor had snitched on him: telling school authorities he's a pedophile and confusing that with being gay.

GD: I wanted to highlight the homophobia that's very

present in Guadeloupe—despite the way Guadeloupeans enjoy cross-dressing during Carnival! But I also wanted to think about snitching, which is also what gets Émilienne's schoolteacher in trouble. Snitching is left over from the slave system, and we shouldn't ever forget what being a slave island has bequeathed to the mind-set of Guadeloupeans. Snitching, I think, is a sick survival strategy, a part of the desire to be seen positively by the white power structure. Hilaire shows us that, as does the self-hating principal who denounces Madame Ladal for her political position and especially for how she nurtures independence in her students.

JM: Are these dead characters, these revenants, your way of nodding to an aesthetic of magical realism?

GD: I suppose it might have that effect on some readers, but honestly it has nothing to do with my literary tastes. The dead are never really dead in Guadeloupe. We speak to them, have lunch in cemeteries to chat with them, and call on our loved ones when we need to. Or sometimes they call on us. My father, for example, came to say goodbye right after the wake, at the point where his soul was leaving to go elsewhere. I could smell his presence in my room. I could feel him in the breeze that came in through the window. So it's no imaginative stretch to have a series of "dead" characters stop in to recount their story and connect it to the churn of the disappearance of the schoolteacher.

JM: There is, of course, one character who is not dead who tells his story, Guy-Albert. I think he's my favorite, probably because he's such a searcher and so sweetly generous.

GD: Guy-Albert, a straightforward worker, is the opposite of the pretentious father, but he's also the character who makes it possible for the father to divest himself of his lack of courage, of his ambiguous patience.

JM: Maybe the alliance between the father and Guy-Albert at the end of the novel—brought about, it seems, through Émilienne's unwitting intervention—is a signal for the reconstruction of Caribbean identity?

GD: That's an interesting way to think about the ending, but in this novel, I wasn't precisely speaking about Caribbean identity. I wanted the novel to be centered on questions of social class. Émilienne's father wants to change his social class, and thus he's bent on rejecting black people who are too poor. He builds his success on others' weakness. What the newfound comradeship between Émilienne's father and Guy-Albert brings up is how class counts and how it can be rethought—something that's not happening very much these days in political discussions among people of color in France.

JM: How so?

GD: Let me give you an example. I was at a conference on diversity in Rouen a few weeks ago, and a film called *The Color Line* was shown. It's all about how young people are suffering because they aren't recognized as being French. One guy, ethnically Chinese but born in France, said the French don't consider Asians to be full human beings. A lot of the black actors interviewed thought they simply represented the exotic other, what they called the "pineapple factor." I found the whole thing sad and even silly. Everybody was talking about a dream of France as a great universalist country. That France doesn't exist. France is built, like every other nation, on inequality. In economics, financial matters, social possibilities, education—inequality is everywhere and particularly present in the lives of people of color! You can't think issues of color without thinking social class. To kill yourself to get to the dream of a country called France presumably based on "liberty, equality, and fraternity" is naive and dangerous.

JM: But don't we need a nation and boundaries in order to have form, in order to feel we exist?

GD: You know, all my life I've been against the idea of a nation, interested instead in the kind of internationalism represented by utopian communism. This return to nationalism that we're feeling everywhere has completely surprised me. I'm stunned to see twenty- and thirty-year-old people being nationalistic (even if they won't use the term). Their way of thinking about living in France is connected to class privilege. It doesn't include any concern for refugees, for example.

JM: Well, you may not be a French or even a Guadeloupean nationalist. But you do communicate in your plays and novels, and especially in *The Restless*, the fabric of Guadeloupean society.

GD: That's because we learn to construct our worlds through the cultures we live in (which is the situation of my characters), but that doesn't mean we can't acquire other lenses.

JM: So let's talk concretely about how you constructed this fiction. I'm fascinated by how you use the Caribbean quadrille to divide up the novel's sections, which also correspond loosely to the three days of the "action," if I can use that term. I've kept the French terms for the dance moves, except for the first one, the waltz. But the others can be understood as a slow movement (*pantalon*), a jumpy strut (*l'été*), a steady repetition (*la poule*), and a kind of lament (*pastourelle*).

GD: Right! The quadrille, which I see you've translated quite correctly as "square dance," is one of those syncretic cultural forms found everywhere there've been massive movements of people from one place to another. We dance the quadrille less now than when I was a girl, but there are still many dance societies that practice a form of disciplined partnering in group formation (as in the European quadrille). The music, of course, is local, changing the beat suddenly, which signals a change in formation. I wanted to use that strategy to think about how the different voices come in as they witness and to determine their intensity, their emotional thrust. I listened to quadrilles while I was writing the novel.

JM: And you've imagined a group caller, instead of one single voice.

GD: Yeah, in the original quadrille, there is *one* caller, traditionally a man. A few women are callers nowadays. But for the novel, I imagined a group of callers made up of both men and women: Émilienne's brothers and sisters control the movement in and out of the courtyard of their spacious bourgeois home, where the voices who visit turn around Émilienne, who is waiting. These circling voices also circle around the country, stopping frequently at the other main location of the novel, La Place de la Victoire, where the strike occurs. Émilienne also has a space, the blue bathroom, where she can try out her real feelings. And she also has to leave the house, which is another way we get to see other sides of Pointe-à-Pitre. She, who is gifted, who can bring forth revenants, helps the readers discover all the dimensions of life in the city, its environs, and even other parts of Guadeloupe. So, we travel from a very tiny blue bathroom to several Guadeloupean towns and villages.

JM: I wanted to ask you about the way you use Creole throughout *The Restless*. I can see the playwright in you in the colloquial language, the quick humor, the snappy remarks, the truculence of the characters. The Creole phrases help locate the novel elsewhere, and so I kept them, sometimes using paraphrasing, sometimes translating into English. What's your own relationship to Creole?

GD: As children we were punished if we used Creole in school, and if people heard us speaking Creole in the streets, they'd tell our parents. I couldn't really speak Creole and, you know, I had to relearn to speak and write it when I returned to Guadeloupe after a prolonged stay in France. In Guadeloupe today, people can and do switch back and forth from French to Creole. This ability to switch is the result of a fight and a political movement to impose Creole everywhere: on TV, on the radio, in meetings, etc. I love to use Creole in my texts. But my writing language is French. I like adding that extra texture, like some Jewish American writers do with Yiddish. And I use Creole whenever it's impossible for my characters to use French to express a precise feeling or thought.

JM: I think one of the intriguing aspects of this novel is how you manage to communicate acts of extreme violence, of terrifying fury, so lightly, so deftly.

GD: I guess you could say I always work towards making my readers and spectators feel the depth of what

I'm saying without indecently vomiting awfulness into their ears. I try to put some distance between my own emotions and how I tell my stories. That's one of the reasons the musicality of my texts is so important to me.

JM: But in your life, outside of writing, you remain pretty direct in your activism, pretty militant.

GD: Now that I'm back in France, I've organized a forum for Caribbean people living in Paris to speak about their concerns, for us to listen to each other's work, to organize. I call it the Senate (*le Sena* in Creole), and we meet every two or three months. I'm also working with a group trying to decolonize the arts, hoping for more representation for people of color, especially on stage and in films.

JM: And you're still trying to make sure that women have "a room of their own"?

GD: All my writing concerns women, violence against them, their need for freedom, their resistance to being confined to "family life." I think I was born a feminist, seeing how difficult it was for women, like my mother, to make a go of it after she divorced my father, with all those kids to take care of. Maybe the happiest I've ever been, certainly the freest, was when I returned alone to Guadeloupe in the eighties as a teacher, living according to the natural rhythms of the island, plunging into politics with other artists and writers. And now I take that energy and put it into my women characters.

JM: Well, Gerty, that energy is not just in your characters!

GD: I know, I think it's in the universe, but you have to grab for it.

The Feminist Press is a nonprofit educational organization founded to amplify feminist voices. FP publishes classic and new writing from around the world, creates cutting-edge programs, and elevates silenced and marginalized voices in order to support personal transformation and social justice for all people.

See our complete list of books at

feministpress.org

FEMINIST
PRESS
AT THE CITY UNIVERSITY
OF NEW YORK